THE SHIFTER'S FIRST BITE

WITCH ISLAND BRIDES, BOOK 3

DEANNA CHASE

BAYOU MOON PRESS, LLC

Welcome to Love Spells, the line of paranormal books where every happily-ever-after comes with a big dose of laughter. Check out all the books in the Love Spells line at www.lovespellsromance.com.

The Shifter's First Bite (Witch Island Brides, Book 3)

Zinnia Franklyn met the love of her life when she was just fifteen years old, and then lost him to Hollywood three years later. Now he's arrived on her island, hotter than ever, and ready to pick up where they left off. There's only one problem… he's supposedly engaged to his costar.

Reed Sinhawk, television star of *Engaged to a Werewolf*, has only ever loved one woman. And the moment he walks back into her life, he's determined to make her his. But will the tabloids, a jealous costar, and his overbearing father succeed in destroying his one chance at happiness?

CHAPTER 1

Zinnia Franklyn stood at her workstation, flexing her cramping hand, and said, "If I have to decorate one more hairy asshole, I'm going to scream."

"That sounds unpleasant," a deep, raspy, all too familiar voice said from behind her.

Zinnia froze. *Oh, no. That did not just happen.* She slowly turned around, and when her gaze landed on the jaw-droppingly sexy werewolf, her heart nearly got caught in her throat. How long had it been since they'd spoken? Twelve, thirteen years? Back then he'd been a tall, gangly teenager with piercing blue eyes and a pretty face just perfect for Teen Wolf magazine. Now he was ruggedly sexy, with broad shoulders, narrow hips, and a five o'clock shadow that would bring any witch to her knees.

Reed Sinhawk, the current television star of *Engaged to a Werewolf*, stood just inside the backroom of her bakery, an amused smile on his chiseled face. He laughed. "Are those the werewolf cookies the production assistant ordered for the set?"

Her face heated as she dropped the pastry bag on the counter and wiped her hands on a towel. The cast of the popular television show were on location on Witch Island for the next couple of months. And while the production assistant had placed the custom bakery order, Zinnia certainly hadn't expected Reed Sinhawk to inquire about them. They weren't even due until much later in the evening. Surely there was some low-level assistant who could've made the trip over to the bakery.

Maybe he'd learned she now lived and worked on the island and had wanted to reconnect with her. The thought had her shaking her head. Why would he do that? He was a television star now, while she was just a bakery owner who specialized in wedding cakes.

"Reed," she said breathlessly as she walked around the table and held her hand out. "It's been a long time. How are you?"

He glanced down at her hand and then raised one eyebrow. "A handshake? Is that all you have for an old friend?"

"I... um..."

"Come here." He held his arms open and gestured with one hand for her to step into his embrace.

She went willingly, breathing in his familiar woodsy scent. The faint forest aroma wasn't one she'd forgotten, and she was instantly transported back to her senior year in high school. They'd been best friends, inseparable for the better part of three years, right up until he'd left for Hollywood and instant stardom. And she'd been left behind, her heart shattered.

"Damn, Zinnia. I missed the hell out of you," he said into her red curls.

"You did?" She pulled back, staring up at him, her eyes wide with shock.

"Of course I did." He gave her a strange look as he dropped his hands to her hips but didn't let go. "What did you think? That I just forgot about the prettiest girl back at Ocean Dunes High?"

"Well... you were busy." She shrugged and stepped back, suddenly feeling as if all the air had left the room. He'd sent her three postcards after he'd left their tiny little town. They'd been filled with the expected excitement of a teenage boy who'd suddenly landed in La La Land. Those cards were still in her keepsake box and had meant so much to her at the time. She'd written pages back, telling him all about the colleges she'd gotten into and how much she missed him. But he'd never responded. That had been the end of their friendship and any girlish dreams that she'd grow up to marry her high school crush.

"Sure," he said with a nod. "But then I guess you were, too, with the end of school and college."

"Right," she said, slightly flustered. She took a full step back, needing some space. Goddess, he was beautiful. Even more beautiful than he'd been at eighteen. She wanted to reach out and touch him again.

When they were in high school, she wouldn't have thought twice about it, but today she kept her hands firmly by her sides. Over a decade had passed, and neither of them were who they'd been back then. "Anyway, that was a long time ago for both of us. I'm sure you didn't stop in here just for a trip down memory lane. Are you here about the cookies? Is there a problem with the order?"

"Nope. I'm definitely not here about the cookies. And to be honest, memory lane is exactly why I stopped in. I overheard the production assistant say your name, and I just had to find out if you were *my* Zinnia." He reached out and wrapped his fingers around hers, his eyes sparkling with amusement as he brought her hand up and gently placed a kiss on her wrist. "Looks like you could use a break. Join me for coffee?"

Zinnia's mouth dropped open. Then she stammered, "Um… You want… coffee?"

"Yeah. I could use a little caffeine and some conversation that doesn't have to do with work. Who better to show me around the island than my old friend from high school?"

Old friend. Yikes. Even though his description was entirely accurate, that wasn't exactly how she wanted to be remembered. She found herself nodding anyway. "Sure. I could do that."

He tucked her arm under his and started to pull her toward the door. "You know a good place?"

She shook her head, trying to clear her fuzzy brain. "We have a coffee pot here."

Reed paused and gazed down at her. "Are you trying to gently brush me off?"

"No! Not at all." Jeez. What was she doing? The hottest man in America, the one she'd loved since she was fifteen years old, had just asked her out to coffee, and she was making a right fool of herself. "Sorry, you just caught me off guard. I wasn't expecting a coffee invitation. Not that I was expecting anything at all. You don't have to do this, you know. Just because we knew each other in high school doesn't mean you have to—"

"Zinnia," he said cutting her off. "I wouldn't have come in if I didn't want to see you."

She quickly clamped her mouth shut, realizing she'd been rambling. A smile tugged at her lips as she took in what he'd said. "Sorry, it's been a long day."

He returned the smile then glanced at the clock, his gray eyes narrowing in focus. "It's not even noon yet."

"Yeah." She let out a nervous chuckle. "I've been working since about four-thirty." Zinnia pulled her apron off and laid it on the counter. After running a hand through her curly red locks, she gave into her temptation and pressed her hand against his chest. "A cup of joe sounds perfect right about now."

His gaze dropped to her hand for just a moment before he returned his focus to her, his grin widening. "You've been up since four-thirty?"

The nonverbal exchange made a tingle shoot

straight to her toes. Trying to pretend as if she hadn't felt a thing, she gave a one shoulder shrug. "No, I was up at a quarter of four. I started working at four-thirty."

"On decorating werewolf assholes?" he asked, giving her a curious look.

Zinnia let out a bark of laughter as she relaxed, feeling as if no time had passed between them. "Yeah, you could say that."

He pulled her toward the front door as he said, "I'm not sure that's what the production assistant had in mind when she ordered werewolf cookies."

"Me neither." She held up one finger, indicating he should wait. Then she ran back into her work room and grabbed one of the cookies. On her way back out, she called to her assistant, "Greta, I'm taking lunch!"

"Okay," her assistant called back.

Zinnia bounced over to Reed, finally recovering from her shock at finding the television star in her store. She held up one of the unfinished cookies. "See this?"

He glanced at it and nodded.

"My sister Frankie—you remember her, right?"

Reed nodded. "Sure. How could I forget? She asked me out on her tenth birthday. Did you know that?"

Zinnia nodded. Her sister had been completely moony-eyed over him. But then, who hadn't? "Yeah. She was heartbroken when you turned her down."

The amusement fled, and his expression turned serious as he said, "I had my eye on someone else."

"You did?" she asked, her throat suddenly dry. "*Who?*" Jealousy rose up and threatened to choke her.

"I'm looking at her," he said with that glint of mischief back in his brilliant blue eyes.

"You did not," she said, smacking his arm and rolling her eyes. There was no way he'd had a thing for her. If he had, why hadn't he ever made a move? He was just messing with her.

"If you say so." He laughed and glanced down at the cookie. "Now what where you saying about those?"

"Oh, right." She cleared her throat. "Frankie did the wolf outlines last night for me. I don't know why she decided to use a wolf showing his backside, but that's what I found in the shop this morning." The wolf was facing away with his tail lifted and his head pointed up in a howl. "I didn't have time to redo them, so I've just been filling in the outline with frosting."

"Please tell me you aren't actually depicting the wolf's... ah, nether region," he said with a grimace.

Laughing, she shook her head and took a bite of the chocolate fudge cookie. "No, just making it look like fur. I don't think actual anatomy would be very appetizing."

"Especially not when they're chocolate." He plucked the cookie from her hand and finished it off in two bites as he followed her out the door.

"Good?" she asked as they strolled down the cobbled streets of Witch Island. The storefronts were decorated with spider webs, enchanted spiders, animated ghosts, ghouls, and goblins, as well as cute pumpkin lights and jack-o-lanterns. Halloween was four weeks away, and the town was already primed for celebration.

"They're better than good. Excellent actually," Reed said. "No one is going to care what they look like once they get a taste."

"Hey! Don't underestimate me," she said, feigning offense. "They'll still look amazing."

"My apologies to the artiste." He winked and pulled open the door to the Caldron Café. Inside the song "Monster Mash" was playing over the sound system. A skeleton standing near the entrance, placed one hand on Reed's shoulder. He jerked back, obviously startled by the movement.

"He's waiting for your jacket," Zinnia said.

Reed stepped away from the skeleton, shrugged out of his sports coat, and handed it over. The skeleton did a twirl and slipped into the jacket, buttoning it in front before he stilled. "Well, that's something I haven't seen before."

"The residents of Witch Island *love* Halloween," Zinnia said, moving backward toward the counter. "Just wait until Halloween night. The town turns into a giant haunted house. It's great."

"It sounds like it." Reed pulled his wallet out of his back pocket and ordered a large black coffee.

Minnie, the barista, gaped at him.

Zinnia waved a hand in front of her friend's face. "Earth to Minnie. Can I get a pumpkin spiced —oomph!"

Someone rammed into Zinnia from behind, slamming her into the counter. An elaborate display of boxed chocolate pumpkins toppled, spilling all over the counter and the floor. "Oh, my gosh," Zinnia huffed out as she immediately started collecting the little boxes and putting them into a pile. "I'm so sorry."

Minnie was still staring over her shoulder, seemingly unconcerned about the chocolate pumpkin massacre.

"Zinnia, are you all right?" Reed said into her ear as his large hands landed gently on her waist.

"Yeah, I think so," Zinnia said as she turned and spotted a small blonde staring at her. Their eyes met and held for just a second, then the woman grabbed onto Reed's arm and said, "Reed, there you are. I've been looking for you all morning. I thought we were going to meet in my room and rehearse that love scene we're supposed to have tonight."

"Krissy, what the hell?" he asked her. "You just knocked my friend over and didn't even apologize."

"Oops," she said, arranging her face into the picture of innocence as she covered her mouth with the tips of her fingers. "My bad. I'm so clumsy sometimes. My apologies. I saw Reed and must not have seen you there."

Sure she hadn't. Zinnia was tall, with long legs, and bright red hair. And while she certainly didn't need to lose weight, she wasn't a waif either. Zinnia took a good look at Krissy Kimble, Reed's co-star. She was tiny, no taller than five-two and not an ounce of extra weight anywhere. She had big blue Kewpie Doll eyes, perfectly straight, shiny hair, and full red lips that matched the thigh-high skirt that showed off her shapely legs and her perfect hourglass figure.

Krissy Kimble was simply gorgeous and made Zinnia feel like something out of *The Night of the Living Dead.* There was no doubt Zinnia had dark circles under her eyes from lack of sleep. She was wearing old frayed jeans, a frosting-stained sweatshirt, and zero make up. On days when she got up way before the crack of dawn and expected to be in the back decorating, she didn't spend much time worrying about her appearance.

Zinnia crossed her arms over her chest and wondered if she could just spell herself to disappear. She probably could, considering she was a witch. The only problem was she had no idea where she'd end up.

"So, about that rehearsal," Krissy was saying to Reed as she ran her fingers over his biceps. "My place? Thirty minutes?"

He grabbed her wrist, stopping her from fondling him. "Not now, Krissy. I'm busy."

"It's okay," Zinnia said, not wanting him to feel obligated to hang out with her if he needed to work. "You don't need to stay for me."

"See, there you go," Krissy said and slipped her arm around Reed, snuggling in close.

Zinnia stared at the two of them. She'd read a while ago that they were an item. It had made sense to her at the time. On screen, they had that sort of magical chemistry that always kept the audience coming back for more. But there in the coffee shop, Reed was stiff and uncomfortable, looking almost as if he wanted to come right out of his skin.

Was there trouble in paradise? Hope welled up inside of her and she immediately mentally chastised herself for thinking she'd ever have a chance with him, glamorous girlfriend or not. Reed was on the island to film a show, not to sweep her off her feet as if she were living in some sort of fairy tale.

Reed grabbed Krissy's wrist and very deliberately removed her arm from his body. He stepped away from her, positioning himself right next to Zinnia. Then, to her surprise, he slipped his hand into Zinnia's and squeezed lightly. "Sorry, Krissy, but since you obviously missed it, let me be clear; I'm on a date with Zinnia here. So, no, rehearsing isn't going to happen. I'll see you tonight at the shoot."

Date? Had he just said date?

Krissy's eyes practically burned holes through Zinnia's skin, and if Reed hadn't been holding on to her, she would've taken a step back just to put distance between them. "Reed," the actress whined, "you know how badly things went last week. I don't want Delaney getting upset. I could really use some rehearsal time. Can't you just reschedule with the townie for tomorrow?"

Townie? What the hell? Had Krissy just popped out of an eighties teen movie? Zinnia opened her mouth to give the uppity actress a piece of her mind, but Reed beat her to the punch.

"Her name is Zinnia," Reed said through clenched teeth. "And no. I won't reschedule. If you want to rehearse, why don't you ask Frank. I'm sure he'd be happy to help you out."

Krissy's face went white as a sheet, then rage flashed in her blue eyes as she clenched her fists, spun around on her heel, and stormed out.

"I take it she isn't a fan of Frank?" Zinnia said just to fill the silence.

"He's a guest star this season and has offered to give her tips more than a few times." He smirked at her. "She didn't appreciate the new guy telling her she could use a little work."

"I can see how that might sting," Zinnia said. "And why she seemed pissed off when you suggested enlisting his help."

"Yeah. I probably shouldn't have said that. Now she's going to be pissed at me." Reed let out an audible sigh. "Sorry about the scene she caused. Are you okay after she nearly knocked you down?"

"I'm fine." Zinnia tried to pull her hand out of his, but he held on and smiled down at her.

"Do you mind?" he asked, nodding to their entwined hands.

"I guess not?" she said, surprised, and making her statement sound more like a question.

"Good. I like it." He winked at her.

She cleared her throat. "Um, I know we just

reconnected and all, and this is not really any of my business, but since you're holding my hand I have to ask. I heard that you and Krissy might be a thing or had been a thing at one point. Am I stepping into the middle of a relationship here?"

"Krissy and I are definitely *not* a thing. Other people would like us to be, but that's never going to happen. Don't worry. I'm single."

"Well, that's a relief," she said. The tension she hadn't even known she'd been holding in her shoulders suddenly melted away.

He smiled at her and then glanced at the barista. "How much do I owe you?"

Minnie rattled off an amount, unable to keep her eyes off him.

"Thanks." He dropped a few bills on the counter, stuffed more in the tip jar, and then handed Zinnia her pumpkin spiced latte. Grabbing his coffee, he asked, "Want to take a walk?"

"Sure." She blinked, wondering if this was really happening. Reed Sinhawk had walked back into her life a half hour ago, and now they were on some sort of date. At least according to him they were. She wished desperately that she would have at least slapped some mascara on before she'd left her house that morning.

Reed led her toward the front door of the café. As the skeleton shed Reed's jacket and gave it back to him, Zinnia glanced over her shoulder at Minnie, her eyes wide with disbelief.

How did this happen? Zinnia mouthed.

No idea, Minnie mouthed back and called after them, "It's a great day for a stroll down by the hot springs. And don't forget, clothes were banned after that die tainted the healing properties!"

Reed turned to look at Minnie. "No-clothes-allowed hot springs? Here on the island?"

She nodded. "They're tucked into the side of the mountain. Great views, and they're perfect on a cool day. Zinnia can show you. She uses them often. Being on her feet all the time is really rough on the body."

Zinnia suddenly imagined what Reed would look like naked. The image of him, all muscles and smooth tanned skin, sent desire to all her girly parts. A small shiver ran through her, and she sucked in a fortifying breath as her face burned for the third time that morning. She glared at her friend and in a snarky tone, she said, "Thanks, Minnie."

"Anytime." Her eyes glinted with mischief as she waved her fingers at them.

Reed nodded and tugged Zinnia back out onto the street. "Well... that was informative."

"You think so?" Zinnia asked.

"Definitely. Are you up for a soak, or do you need to get back to work?" He still had ahold of her hand and didn't seem in any hurry to give it back. When she glanced up at him, she saw his eyes had darkened with undeniable desire. Her entire body started to tingle from head to toe.

Zinnia still had about three dozen cookies to decorate. If she was a responsible witch, she'd decline

Reed's invitation. But who was she kidding? She was single and hadn't been out on a date in over nine months. And here was her first love, the gorgeous television star Reed Sinhawk, staring at her like he wanted to eat her alive.

She had no choice in the matter, and without making a conscious decision, she felt herself nodding as her lips formed the words, "Yes. I'd love to take a soak."

CHAPTER 2

"This way." Zinnia led her hot celebrity down the narrow, wooded path, her heart hammering with anticipation. She couldn't quite believe she was doing this. She hadn't seen or heard from him in years. Plus, they'd only been friends back then, and yet, instead of taking him to the area that had individual private springs, she'd chosen the path that would take them to Lover's Cove, the larger springs that were big enough for two people and had a stunning view of Silver Bay.

She blamed him and the way he kept looking at her. How was she supposed to keep her hormones in check when she was certain he was imagining what it would be like to rip her clothes off with his bare teeth?

"It's better at night when the moon is shining off the water," Zinnia said. "But daytime soaking has its advantages too."

"No doubt," he said from behind her, his voice a little growly.

A shiver of anticipation rolled through her and she briefly glanced back. He gave her a wolfish smile that told her everything she needed to know about his state of mind. He'd finally dropped her hand when they'd stepped onto the narrow path, but that hadn't stopped the electricity sparking between them. She could feel his every movement with each step she took.

Finally, when they rounded a large pine tree, she saw the unlit marker for the spring, indicating it was free. Butterflies sprang to life in her stomach. This was really happening. *Oh goddess, how was this happening?* Zinnia wasn't the type of person to get naked in front of a man on their first date. But this was Reed Sinhawk, and he wasn't exactly a stranger. At one time, she'd known everything there was to know about him except what it felt like to be wrapped in his arms naked. And that was something she'd regretted for the last decade.

Zinnia paused by the marker, her fingers hovering over the button. If she touched it, she was really going through with this. If she didn't—

Reed slid his hand over hers and gently pressed the button. The marker lit up with a soft blue glow. "Ready?" he asked.

His warm hand calmed her nerves. She smiled at him. "Ready."

He narrowed his eyes and really studied her. "Are you sure? You seemed to hesitate there for a minute."

She stepped up to him and pressed a soft hand to his chest. "I'm sure."

That wolfish smile returned, and he brushed a lock of her hair out of her eyes. Then without saying a word, he grabbed her hand and took the lead down the path.

Zinnia had to quicken her pace to keep up with him and almost ran right into him when he came to an abrupt stop.

"Whoa," he said quietly as he gazed out at the water crashing on the rocks below. "This is…"

"Breathtaking," Zinnia said. The view never failed to enchant her and was half the reason she frequented the springs.

He glanced down at her. "Just like you."

"Oh come on." She laughed and rolled her eyes. "That was cheesy as hell. Did you get that from a script?"

His lips twitched with amusement. "You're questioning the integrity of my seduction techniques?"

"Yes." Still laughing, she shook her head and walked over to the edge of the pool. The natural spring had been lined with slate and was fed by a small waterfall. Everything about it was straight out of a fairytale, including the man standing next to her. Suddenly she felt as if her current reality was too good to be true. She turned to Reed. "Why did Krissy want to rehearse your love scene? I've seen your show. It's not like you haven't had to do them together before."

He glanced from Zinnia to the spring and back to

Zinnia. Both of his eyebrows shot up. "Krissy isn't exactly the topic I want to discuss right now."

She placed her hands on her hips. "I'm sure she isn't, but I saw the way she looked at us when she noticed we were holding hands. Does she have a thing for you?"

"Does it matter if she does? We're not together."

"Did you date before?" Zinnia didn't know why she was pressing him on this. It had been obvious from their interaction that they weren't together, and he'd flat out told Krissy that he and Zinnia were on a date. And she wasn't under any illusions that this was going to be anything more than a hot fling. Reed was on the island for a few months, and then he'd go back to Hollywood with the rest of the cast.

"No." He shrugged out of his sports coat.

"Reed," she pressed, "I read you two were an item in an article somewhere. Something about an impending engagement."

He let out an irritated sigh. "That was leaked to the press by our parents. Both of our fathers are eager for us to make our television relationship into the real thing."

"They are? Why?" Zinnia asked, standing frozen as she watched him reach behind his shoulders and tug his long-sleeved henley over his head.

"Family dynasties," he said with a shrug. "Her dad wants an in with my father for his political connections, while my father wants some sort of connection to hers for big business opportunities. It's bullshit, and I want nothing to do with it."

"I see," she said faintly as she stared at his well-defined chest. The man had muscles for days, and it was all she could do to keep herself from petting him.

He started to undo the button of his jeans.

Zinnia's gaze was riveted, and when his zipper came down, she sucked in a breath.

Reed chuckled. "Are you going to join me in the spring, Zinnia?"

"Huh?" She finally tore her gaze from his body and met his eyes.

"The spring? Are you going in, or should I turn this little display into a strip show?"

"Oh, crap. I'm sorry," she said, mortified as she kicked her shoes off. "I guess I got a little caught up. It's not every day I see someone... um, someone like you taking his clothes off."

His blue-gray eyes glittered with mischief as he said, "And here I'd hoped that because we'd been friends you at least watched my show."

"Oh, I do," she said, shrugging out of her sweatshirt. "It's just that seeing you in the flesh is a lot more satisfying."

He dropped his pants, leaving him in his boxer briefs.

She swallowed, trying to look anywhere other than the obvious bulge in his shorts.

"Turn around," he said.

"Why?"

"Because I'm going to finish getting undressed, and

when I'm done, I'm going to get into that pool. Then I'll turn around and let you have your privacy."

Zinnia widened her eyes in surprise. He was the same sweet, thoughtful guy he'd been back in high school, and her heart swelled with the realization that Hollywood hadn't turned him into someone completely different. She smiled and turned her back to him. "You got it."

A few moments passed, then she heard the faint lapping of the water right before he said, "Okay. Your turn."

Peeking over her shoulder, Zinnia found him in the pool, waist deep, staring at the waterfall. She'd have been happy to stand there gazing at his muscular shoulders, but he cleared his throat and said, "You coming?"

"Yep!" She quickly stripped out of her jeans, T-shirt, and underclothes and let out a small cry as a gust of wind blew off the water, chilling her to the bone. "Oh my goddess, that's cold."

"Then get your cute ass in here where it's warm," he ordered.

Zinnia rushed into the pool and sank down to her shoulders, letting out a sigh of relief. "Damn, that feels good."

"Is it safe to turn around now?" he asked.

She chuckled, both grateful and amused at his chivalry. "Yes. Thank you."

The water rippled with his movement as he faced her. His gaze slowly swept over her face and bare shoulders, appreciation lighting his eyes. "You look gorgeous."

"You can barely see anything," she said with an eye roll, secretly loving his flattery. Who didn't want to be admired by a man so gorgeous he likely could have any woman he wanted?

"I can see enough." He held his hand out. "Come over here. You're too far away."

As much as she was enjoying being around him, now that they were both naked in the pool, Zinnia was starting to have second thoughts on just how far she wanted this outing to go. She shook her head. "I think it's best if we each stay on our own sides of the pool."

Something that looked a lot like regret flickered in his eyes before he shrugged one shoulder and sat down on the small ledge that ringed the pool. "Sure."

She scooted back, finding her own ledge, and kicked her feet out in front of her. Only her foot connected with his leg, and due to the buoyancy of the water, her foot kept going, sliding up his thigh and toward the promised land.

"Whoa there," he said softly, catching her foot with his hands. "Don't want to knock anything out of commission."

"Oops, sorry. That wasn't intentional," she said, trying unsuccessfully to pull her foot away.

"No apology necessary." He tightened his grip and started to knead the bottom of her foot with his knuckles.

"Mmmm," she moaned, her eyes closing reflexively

as her head fell back. "You have no idea how good that feels."

"If the look on your face is any indication, I think I have some idea." The hand that had been holding her in place started to drift up her ankle and over her calf.

His touch was making her tingle all over, and another moan came from deep in her throat. She started to wonder why she'd decided they needed to sit so far apart. Not that she was complaining about her current situation.

"Zinnia, if you make that sound again, I think I'm going to lose my mind," he said in that deep, raspy voice that had made millions of American women fall in lust with him over the last few years.

She tilted her head up and opened her eyes. That wolfish look was back, and every part of her came alive with wanting. Her resolve to stay on her side of the pool vanished, and Zinnia gently pulled her foot out of his grasp. Without a word, she drifted over and straddled him, her boldness surprising even herself. His hands immediately rested on her hips as hers circled his neck.

Steam rose in the cool air around them as they just stared at each other. Reed's gaze fixated on her lips, and she couldn't help but lean into him. Years of longing rushed to the surface, pulling her to him, invading her entire body with want and need.

He slid one hand slowly up her side, stopping just before he cupped her bare breast. Still staring at her lips, he asked, "Are you sure this is what you want?

Because if you say yes, I'm going to kiss you all over and I might never stop."

A shot of desire went straight to her center as she breathed, "I'm sure."

"Thank the gods," he said as he tightened his grip on her and went straight for her neck, kissing, tasting, teasing. He all but devoured her and laved at her pulse with determined intensity. Suddenly Zinnia couldn't take it anymore. She pulled back, pressed both of her hands to his cheeks, and crushed her lips to his.

He tasted faintly of chocolate and coffee and pure lust. She decided right then that she could be happy kissing him forever. But then he pulled back, lightly scraping his teeth over her lips, and a vivid image of him using those teeth to pleasure her in other ways flashed in her mind. She wanted more. Much more. She scooted closer, reveling in the weight of his excitement pressing into her belly and—"

"Reed! What are you doing?" a woman's shrill voice called.

Zinnia froze.

Reed swore.

Zinnia scrambled off Reed's lap, crossing her arms over her chest as she sank as far into the water as she could. Krissy was standing at the edge of the pool, her hands on her hips and a scowl on her face.

"Do you have any idea what this is going to do to the ratings if the gossip rags get ahold of this? You can't be out in public hooking up with every random celebrity stalker you find. For the love of the gods,

Reed. Don't you ever think before you get yourself into these situations?"

"Hey, I'm not a celebrity stalker! Reed and I have known each other for years," Zinnia said, nearly coming right out of the water before she realized she was still completely naked. Then mortification rendered her silent as she watched a man pop up behind Krissy and snap photo after photo of her, Reed, and their clothes scattered on the stone path.

Krissy's mouth formed a shocked "O" as she spun around. "Dammit! What did you do, follow me?"

"You said you wanted pictures. How else was I supposed to get them?" the beady-eyed weasel of a man asked.

"I—what? I didn't… Reed, I did not ask this man for pictures!" Her face was scrunched up with righteous indignation. Zinnia couldn't help but conclude that her performance was good enough for a best actress nomination.

"Cut the crap, Krissy." Reed's body vibrated with pure anger as he stalked out of the pool. "Do you really expect me to believe you had no idea he was there?"

Beads of water glistened on his god-like naked body as he reached over and grabbed the camera out of the man's hands. Without a word, he threw it over the cliff.

"Hey, jackass. You can't do that!" The man's face turned red with anger as he rushed over to the edge of the mountain. "It's gone! You're gonna pay for that."

Relief washed over Zinnia. The idea of seeing

herself naked in a tabloid made her want to vomit. But Reed had saved the day by destroying the evidence.

Reed glared at the man. "Get out of here, or I'll call the authorities and have you hauled out."

The photographer stalked back toward the path, and as he passed Krissy, he said, "You still owe me my fee."

Her face went ghostly-white, but then she straightened her shoulders and said, "I have no idea what you're talking about."

"You just keep telling yourself that, lady. My bill will be in your inbox by the end of the day." His boots clattered on the slate stones and everyone was silent until the sound of his footsteps finally faded away.

Reed turned on Krissy, his voice barely audible when he asked, "Why did you do this?"

"I…" She glanced over at Zinnia, who was still huddled in the water wishing she could vanish into thin air. "I didn't know you were with her."

"You saw us together at the coffee shop," Zinnia said, finally finding her voice. "Reed told you we were on a date. What else did you think you were going to find?"

Krissy took a step closer to the pool and glared at Zinnia. "You two *just* met. How was I supposed to know you were going to throw yourself at him?"

"Enough!" Reed barked. "Not that it's any of your business, but as Zinnia already told you, we've known each other for years. She's one of my oldest friends.

And that's all I'm going to say about that. Now leave, Krissy. You don't belong here."

She turned her oh-so-innocent eyes on him. "I just came to tell you that the shooting time has been moved up. You need to be on set in an hour."

He reached down and pulled his phone out of his pants. After taking a second to study the screen, he narrowed his eyes at her. "That's a lie. Delaney would've called me."

"Delaney dropped her phone and it died," she said with an air of satisfaction. "So I told her I'd track you down. And isn't it fortunate that I did. Don't want to waste production money now, do we?" She sent Zinnia a twisted, self-satisfied smile, then turned on her heel and headed toward the path that led back to the parking area. She took two steps, and thanks to the water that Reed had dripped on the stones, her fancy Louboutin slipped right out from under her and the actress went tumbling sideways into the bushes lining the path. Her feet, adorned with her two red-soled shoes, stuck out just like the Wicked Witch of the East from the *Wizard of Oz*.

Zinnia snickered and quickly clamped her hand over her mouth when Reed glanced her way.

He sent her an amused smile as he took the time to pull on his boxers, jeans, and henley shirt. Then he strode over and offered a hand to his co-star who was still struggling to free herself from the bushes.

Once Krissy was back on her feet, she emerged from the foliage with leaves in her hair and the bottom of her skirt caught on her slim black belt, leaving her bare ass exposed. Zinnia couldn't help but notice the many fresh scratches and scrapes from her unfortunate tangle with the branches.

"No underwear?" Zinnia said, unable to control her laughter. "Good thing the paparazzi already left, huh?"

"Dammit!" Krissy quickly pulled her skirt down, straightened her shoulders, and took a careful deliberate step toward the path.

"Wait," Reed called.

She paused and looked at him with hopeful eyes.

"You have something in your hair." Reed reached over and plucked the green vine out of her tangled blond locks. "There. All set."

Krissy scowled at him. "This is your fault."

"My fault? Are you high? I just wanted a soak in the hot springs with the town's engaging wedding cake baker. You're the one who followed us out here and brought a fucking photographer. No, Krissy, you don't get to pin this on me."

She cut her gaze to Zinnia and then back to him. "You and I both know if you'd just have come back with me when I saw you at the coffee—"

"Go. Now!" He pointed to the trail. "I'll see you at the set when I'm damned well good and ready."

There must've been something in his tone that finally resonated with her, because the television star turned and, without a word, stalked off down the path, limping slightly as she went.

He ran a frustrated hand through his hair and turned back to Zinnia. "I'm really sorry about that."

"It's not your fault." She glanced around at the clouds rolling in. "I should probably get dressed and get back to the shop. I still have work to do."

"Right." But he didn't turn around. He just stood there, watching her, a troubled look on his face.

"Reed?" she asked with a small smile.

"Yeah?"

"Think you could turn around again?"

His gaze dropped once again to her bare shoulders and there was no mistaking the regret in his expression. Then he blinked and said, "Right. Of course."

Once he turned his back to her, Zinnia braced herself and climbed out of the pool. The cold air hit her and made her teeth chatter. If she'd been thinking at all or had planned this trip to the springs, she'd have brought her enchanted self-heating towels and a couple of robes. But she'd been in too big of a hurry to get her hands on Reed for that idea to even cross her mind.

"Son of a…" Reed grabbed his sports jacket, and while still looking away, he handed it back to her. "Here, use this."

"It's… okay," she said with a stutter.

"Zinnia, please. Your teeth are going to chatter right out of your head." He turned around and draped the coat over her shoulders. Instead of leaving her to get dressed, he stood behind her, rubbing his hands up and down her arms, trying his best to warm her.

"Thanks." She let out a sigh of relief as her shivering stopped, and she was finally able to call up her magic. Holding both hands straight out toward the ocean, she said, "From the sun and moon and my witches' worth, I call the warmth from the depths of the earth."

Heat radiated from the ground and swirled around her, instantly drying her wet body.

"Wow. That would've been handy ten minutes ago, before I threw my clothes back on," Reed said.

"There are perks to being a witch." She glanced over her shoulder. "If the situation had been different, I'd have definitely shared that perk with you." Clutching the coat around her, she stepped out of his hands and quickly redressed. When she was done, she handed the coat back to him and held out her hand. "Let's go, T.V. star. We both have places to be."

He let out a small groan but took her hand in his and let her lead him back to reality.

CHAPTER 3

R eed barely knocked before he barged into Krissy's dressing room. The drive from town to the big house on the hill where they were filming had done little to calm his temper. He still couldn't believe that she'd followed him and Zinnia to the hot springs with that photographer in tow. What in the devil's name had she been thinking? She was up to something; he just didn't know what.

"Krissy!" he called, slamming the door. Her framed headshot rattled against the shaking wall.

"In here," she called back from the room's en suite bathroom.

"Get out here. We need to talk." He paced the length of the room, too wound up to sit.

"Ugh. Hold on. I'm having an… issue." Her whiney tone grated on his nerves.

He'd woken that morning with Zinnia on his mind. Reed had first heard her name the night before and had grilled the production assistant on what she'd looked like. Zinnia was an unusual name, but he had no reason to believe the woman the PA had seen was *his* Zinnia, the girl he'd left behind thirteen years ago. They hadn't lived on Witch Island then, and the chances of finding her here seemed impossible. But then he'd walked into her bakery and there she was, her bright blue eyes sparkling at him. Her eyes had haunted his dreams for years, eyes he'd searched for in a crowd more times than he could count.

He glanced around, scanning for the bottle of scotch he knew Krissy usually kept around. But the small booze cart that had last been near the loveseat was missing. "Where's the scotch?"

"Gone. I threw it out." She emerged from the bathroom in a short silk robe with a pained expression on her face and pink lotion all over her arms and thighs.

He frowned. "What's that? Some new skin treatment?"

Krissy shook her head. "I have a rash and—" She grimaced and shifted uncomfortably from foot to foot. "It's all over my legs, butt, and... other places. I think it's poison ivy."

He raised one eyebrow. "Other places? Does that mean what I think it means?"

She rocked her hips from side to side and looked like she was going to cry.

Pity cooled his temper as he imagined what it would be like to have a poison ivy rash in his crotch area. It wasn't something he'd wish on his worst enemy. "Ouch. That's gotta suck."

"You have no idea." One single tear rolled down her cheek as she stood there awkwardly, seemingly unsure of what to do with herself.

"You can't sit down, can you?" he asked, eyeing her stiff stance.

"No. I have Calamine lotion, but I can't put it *down there*."

"That's... well, I'm sorry to hear that." He stared at her, taking in her glassy eyes and pouty lips. "Obviously we can't film today's scene while you're in this state. I'll go let Delaney know that you're out of commission." He started to move toward the door. As much as he still wanted to chew her out for her actions earlier in the day, he didn't have it in him to kick her when she was down.

"That's it? You're just leaving me here like this?" she asked, going from pathetic to outraged in two seconds flat.

"What else am I supposed to do?" he asked through clenched teeth, tired of her bullshit. How many more weeks was it before the show wrapped for the season? Too many as far as he was concerned. But at least he'd be on the island and near Zinnia. He was counting the hours until he could see her again. They had unfinished business to attend to.

"You're a mean bastard, Reed Sinhawk. Do you know that? Are you really just going to leave after finding me like this? Don't you have any chivalry left?"

Reed rolled his eyes. Talk about a drama queen. "You have a rash, Krissy, not some mysterious, flesh-eating virus."

"It hurts to even breathe," she said with a whimper. Her lower lip trembled, and the misery in her big blue eyes hit him somewhere in the gut. She really was in pain.

Reed held his hand out. "Come here."

She glanced at his hand, held hers up, and shook her head. "It's covered in lotion."

"I can see that now." She really was a mess. "Okay, do you think you can sit in the car?"

She shook her head.

He eyed her, contemplating his next move. She needed a healer. Reed pulled his phone out of his pocket and called Delaney.

"Where are you two?" the assistant director asked, sounding hurried and distracted as usual.

"We have a problem," Reed said. "Krissy needs a healer as soon as possible. Do we have one on location with us?"

"What's wrong?" Her tone was instantly sharp and fully focused.

"She seems to have lost a fight with some poison ivy and it's everywhere. There's no way we can do the scene today until she gets some relief."

"Son of a... dammit." There was a rustling over the connection followed by another curse.

"Delaney?" he asked. "You still there?"

"The healer we hired flaked at the last minute. He

36

took a job with that weirdo Corey Curses. One hundred shows in a hundred days or something ridiculous like that."

"You mean the witch who hands out curses for entertainment, Vegas style? Didn't he give an entire audience flatulence once and the city had to shut down due to the toxic stench?"

"That's the one," Delaney said. "Apparently he pays three times what we do."

Reed wrinkled his nose. "I guess he'd have to with that kind of workload. Besides the pay, it sounds like a stinky job."

Delaney groaned, and Reed chuckled, amused at his childish pun.

"Excuse me," Krissy said, rubbing her thighs together in an awkward fashion. "Anyone remember me?"

"Right. Of course." Reed sobered and spoke into the phone. "So, no healer on staff, but there must be one in town, right?"

"Of course." Delaney rattled off a phone number. "Her name is Mystia, and she's already on retainer. Call me back as soon as you know anything, and we'll see if we can salvage any of the filming schedule today."

"I'm on it." Reed ended the call and tapped in the number for the healer.

"Witch Island Holistic Center. How can I help you?"

"Good afternoon," Reed said. "I'm looking for the healer, Mystia."

"She's with a patient right now. Can I get your

name, number, and what you need help with? I can get her to return your call just as soon as she's done."

Reed explained the situation and then asked, "Can she come here? Krissy is having trouble sitting in the car."

"Poison ivy all over. That's a tricky one," the assistant said. "I'm sure Mystia is going to want her here. We have a tub just for rashes. I'd say it's best to bring your friend in. I can get the bath ready while you're on your way."

Reed glanced at Krissy again. Everything was red and swollen, and she was fidgeting like a nervous cat. Waiting for the healer would just mean she'd suffer longer. "Okay, we're on our way."

"Excellent, Mr. Sinhawk. We'll be ready." The line went dead, and Reed stuffed his phone into his pocket.

"Okay, Krissy. Let's go." He waved for her to follow him.

"I can't." Her voice was so low, he barely heard her.

He paused and glanced over at her. She was doing an odd little dance, grinding her butt against a table while scratching her neck with one hand and rubbing her crotch with the other. He blinked. Her expression turned to one of bliss that was quickly replaced with a grimace as she scratched her neck harder.

"Krissy. Don't!" he ordered.

"You have no idea how much it itches. I can't stop." She started to pant, still grinding her backside against the table edge.

Holy hell, he thought. She was going to rub herself

raw and not in the good way. He had to do something. His mind flashed back to when he was a boy and had caught a case of the chicken pox. The itching had been horrendous, and the only way he'd kept from skinning himself alive was when his mother had duct taped mittens on his hands. He wasn't going to find mittens in her dressing room. But socks would work. Reed strode over to her bureau and started rummaging around.

"Hey," she said half-heartedly. "Don't paw through my panties."

"Trust me. That's the last thing I want to do," he said. She let out a huff of annoyance. Or was that offense? He didn't know and didn't care. His only goal was to get her to stop scratching. If she ended up with scars, she'd be devastated and then madder than a shifter on fire. He finally found what he was looking for in the last drawer and pulled out a pair of thick socks. "Okay," he said as he strode over to her. "Give me one of those hands."

"No." She shook her head violently and continued to scratch her chest then hopped on one leg as she reached for her foot. If he didn't know better, he'd think she was possessed by a flesh-eating demon.

"Krissy, you're going to hurt—"

Before he could even finish his sentence, she lost her balance, knocked over a floor lamp, and went down in an impressive heap of arms and legs. Her robe had flipped up, leaving her bare ass exposed and looking like something out of a horror movie. Her skin was bright red, and blisters had already started to appear. He winced, his entire body shuddering with sympathy.

"Damn, Krissy," he said quietly as he crouched down. "You sure did a number on yourself."

She just lay there whimpering as he slipped the socks over her hands. Then she looked up at him with tears in her eyes. "I'm sorry. I shouldn't have followed you."

"No, you shouldn't have," he said and reached down to gingerly pick her up. She let out a groan but let him shift her in his arms so that she was cradled against his chest. "Is this okay?"

She closed her eyes and nodded, bravely trying to act as if she wasn't in agony. But there was no hiding the pain etching her face.

His chest ached with sympathy, and without another word, he carried her to the car and gently laid her in the back seat of his rented 4Runner. Ten minutes later, he carried her into the healer's office and said, "We need help."

"What seems to be the problem?" the receptionist asked.

Krissy lifted her head and cried, "I have boils on my ass and they're spreading to my vajayjay!"

CHAPTER 4

Zinnia hurried into the holistic center, clutching her hand to her abdomen. She'd been daydreaming about Reed and had let a cookie cutter get away from her, resulting in a flesh wound that required some attention. It wasn't dire, but she couldn't go back to work while bleeding all over everything.

"Zinnia, what happened?" Nissa, the receptionist, asked as she walked up to the desk.

"I had a fight with a cookie cutter and lost," she said, holding up her hand that was wrapped in a blood-soaked towel.

"Okay. Wait right here." Nissa got to her feet. "I'll let Mystia know, and then I'll be right back."

"Thanks," Zinnia said and leaned against the desk.

"Oh. My. Goddess. Did you see who just walked through here?" someone asked from the waiting area.

Zinnia glanced over and spotted Lenora, the town's

notoriously bad matchmaker. "No. I was too busy trying not to bleed all over everything."

Lenora dropped her gaze to Zinnia's hand and grimaced. "Ouch. That looks bad. But this should cheer you up. I just saw Reed Sinhawk and that woman, Krissy something, come in. They're with Mystia right now." She lowered her voice and stage-whispered, "It sounded like she has some sort of venereal disease. I heard her say something about a rash spreading from her buns to her kitty cat. That can't be good."

"She has an STD?" Zinnia blurted out. And if so, why the heck had Reed brought her in? Wasn't that a little… personal? He'd said they hadn't dated, but had they hooked up? Her mind whirled with suspicions, and she wondered if she'd just dodged a bullet.

Lenora rose from her seat and moved to stand next to Zinnia. "Isn't it just so romantic how they're meant for each other."

"STDs aren't romantic, Lenora," Zinnia said, closing her eyes. The man she'd been making out with less than two hours ago had just brought his co-star into the clinic for an STD. He'd only do that if he was involved, right? Humiliation settled in her bones and made her want to kick something. Or someone named Reed. How could she be so naïve? Had everything he'd said been an act? Or did he have some sort of friends-with-benefits relationship with Krissy? Her stomach turned at the thought of being lied to.

"Jackass," Zinnia mumbled under her breath as she

unconsciously curled her fingers into a fist. Pain shot through her hand and up her arm, making her stifle a groan. Dammit, she'd been so caught up in her thoughts about Krissy and Reed she'd almost forgotten about her cut.

"I read last week in Shifter magazine that they've been destined to be together since birth," Lenora continued as if Zinnia hadn't just sworn for no apparent reason. "Isn't it interesting that in this day and age a pseudo-arranged marriage actually seems to be working out? When I read about it, I thought that was creepy. Who wants their parents to pick their lover?" The woman gave a visible shudder. "And even though they seem to be having some sort of private issue when it comes to the bedroom, it's obvious they are meant for each other. They're a perfect match. You should've seen the love that was wrapped around them like a cocoon. I couldn't have found them better matches if I'd tried."

Zinnia didn't trust Lenora's judgement on love matches any more than she did Reed at the moment, but the comment about seeing love wrapped around them made her give Lenora a second glance. "You saw their love for each other?"

"Oh, yes. It's sapphire blue, indicating deep affection. When you see couples like that, they almost never break up. Lifers is what I call them." She grinned. "I can't wait to watch them get married on that show of theirs. Will you be making the cake?"

"Yes," Zinnia said flatly. She wanted to beat her head against the wall. How had she fallen for his bullshit about how they weren't together? Of course they were. They had a show called *Engaged to a Werewolf*. On top of that, she'd been stupid to believe that he'd have any sort of feelings for her after all the years that had passed. If he'd wanted to find her, to get in touch, it would've been simple enough. And it would've had to be him who reached out to her. He was far too insulated for her to just pick up the phone and call him. She'd been played. There was no doubt about it.

"Zinnia?" Nissa called, poking her head out from the back. "Mystia has a few minutes to patch up that hand now."

"Coming." She strode forward and followed Nissa back into the exam area, more than ready to end the conversation about Reed and Krissy. She braced herself, praying she wouldn't run into either of them. To her relief, Nissa opened one of the exam rooms and waved her in.

"Mystia will be right with you." She smiled and closed the door.

Almost immediately, Mystia appeared. Her dark curly hair was swept up into a messy bun, and she had something that looked like a ketchup stain on her white lab coat. Or was that blood?

Zinnia frowned. "Busy day?"

"You have no idea," the healer said. "Now, let's see what you've done to yourself."

Mystia gingerly took Zinnia's hand and gently unwrapped the towel. The wound immediately started to well with blood. "Oh, yeah. You're definitely going to need stitches."

Zinnia groaned. "I was hoping some of your magic skin glue would do the trick."

"Sorry. Not this time. But the stitches have been spelled for rapid healing. Two, three days and you'll be as good as new."

"Well, that's something," Zinnia said. "What about water? Can I get it wet?" With her work, not washing her hands wasn't an option.

"Yep. Water is fine as long as you take the herbs I prescribe. They keep infection at bay." Mystia got to work on flushing the wound. While she cleaned the cut, she ran her magic-filled fingertips over Zinnia's skin. Magical light shimmered and clung to Zinnia's flesh, numbing the area. The healer glanced up at the patient. "Feeling better?"

Zinnia tried to flex her hand and felt nothing. "Much," she said with a sigh of relief. "I hadn't even realized how much it was throbbing before you did that."

"It's the adrenaline. This should be easy to stitch. I'm going to go grab my sutures. Hold tight. I'll be back." The healer swept out of the room, leaving Zinnia on the table.

The clock ticked loudly in the silent room, and when five minutes went by, Zinnia started to get restless while her bladder got impatient. She got up off the table and poked her head out the door. There was a murmur of voices from an exam room a couple of doors down and a unisex restroom at the end of the hall.

Zinnia glanced around for Mystia, and when she didn't spot her, she scurried off to the bathroom. A few minutes later she popped back out, intending to head straight to her exam room, but the voices stopped her in her tracks.

"Oh, yes. Right there," the familiar female said with a moan. Krissy. Zinnia would know that high pitched voice anywhere. "More. More!" she demanded. "Oh, goddess, yes, that's it."

"God, Krissy," Reed said and then groaned.

Zinnia's stomach turned, and she pressed her good hand to her mouth, fearing she'd get sick right there in the hallway. Were they really doing what it sounded like they were doing? And while they were in to get an STD checked? What kind of kinky crap were those two into? She started to scurry back to her room but froze when she heard Mystia's voice.

"That's good," Mystia said. "Continue spreading the cream over her back, and once it covers the rash, help her into the healing bath. Okay? I've got another patient who's waiting, but I'll be back as soon as I'm done."

Rash? Back? Healing cream? Zinnia blinked. That didn't sound anything like an STD. A small bubble of laughter escaped her lips just as the door swung open, and Mystia swept out of the room.

"Zinnia," the healer said, surprised. "Were you looking for me?"

"No… I was just coming from the restroom," she said, waving awkwardly behind her.

"Zinnia?" Reed's voice floated from the exam room, followed by heavy footsteps.

"Reed? Wait, come back. I think you missed a spot," Krissy called.

He was out the door before Zinnia could escape to the safety of her own exam room. "Hey," he said, concern shining in his eyes. "What happened?"

"Cookie cutter accident," she said with a sheepish smile. Then she glanced at the exam room behind him. "And what brings you here?"

He glanced over his shoulder. "Krissy. Remember when she fell into the bushes back at the springs?"

She nodded. "Sure. How could I forget?"

"Well, it turns out she wrestled with a poison ivy plant, but Mystia here is fixing her up."

"Reed!" Krissy called from the room. "I *need* you."

He groaned, the same type of groan she'd heard earlier and had mistaken for one of pleasure. It wasn't. He looked anything but happy at the moment. "Sorry. I've got to get back in there and calm the drama queen."

"Sure," Zinnia said, wondering how he had the patience to deal with his costar. Zinnia would've lost her mind by now.

"If you're up to it, maybe you could come by the set

later?" he asked. "I'd really like to catch up with you and find out what you've been doing all these years."

She shrugged. "I've just been baking. Not much to tell."

He swept his gaze over her then shook his head. "I'm not buying it. Thirteen years is a long time, Zin. I know you've got at least a few stories for me."

Zin. It's what he'd used to call her back in the day. Her resolve melted, and she found herself nodding. "Okay. I have to drop off the cookies anyway."

"Good." He reached out and squeezed her good hand and then disappeared back into the exam room.

"It took you long enough!" she heard Krissy say.

Mystia raised both eyebrows and gestured to Zinnia's room. "Ready?"

"You have no idea." Zinnia followed her, and once she was back on the exam table, she blew out a long breath.

"You can say that again," Mystia said, gently taking another look at Zinnia's wounded hand.

Zinnia blinked. "Crazy day?"

"Not as crazy as yours," she said with a soft chuckle.

"Huh?" Zinnia glanced down at her hand.

"I just mean that it's not every day a handsome television star looks at a girl like that. Whatever he has planned for later, I think it's certain romance is in your future."

Zinnia glanced away, heat crawling up her neck. "That's not…" She shook her head. "You're reading too much into it."

"Am I?" Mystia laughed again. "We'll see." She winked then turned serious as she reached for the wounded hand. "Ready for me to stitch this up?"

Zinnia nodded, her mind already running away from her as she imagined being back in Reed's arms. A small smile tugged at her lips and five minutes later, without her even noticing, her hand was stitched.

CHAPTER 5

Z innia balanced the pink bakery boxes in both
hands and carefully maneuvered down the
narrow hallway of the old Victorian mansion that now
served as the set for *Engaged to a Werewolf.* An assistant
had let her in and pointed her toward the parlor room
that was apparently somewhere in the back of the 9000
square foot home.

The place had been on the island for over two
hundred years and was a landmark. Six months ago, it
had been sold to some LLC and completely remodeled.
No one knew who owned it, but whoever it was had
clearly demanded perfection. The place was gorgeous
with crown molding, wainscoting, fresh paint,
gleaming hardwood floors, and gorgeous antiques
everywhere. There was no doubt it would shine as the
backdrop to the show's fourth season.

The hallway opened up into what had to be a

ballroom. There were two hallways, one toward the back of the room on the right and the other on the left.

"Okay, now where?" Zinnia asked herself. She glanced down both, seeing nothing particularly identifying, and then took the closest one, the hallway on the right. Electric light flickered from ornate candelabras, illuminating the portraits of characters from the show.

One depicted Reed and Krissy, their heads together as they both gazed at the giant rock on her ring finger. And even though Zinnia knew the image was one from the show, it still made her stomach turn to see them together. Seeing Reed after all the years that had passed, had awakened something in her she thought she'd long gotten over. Her feelings for him hadn't ever faded, they'd just been buried.

She sighed. This couldn't be healthy. Maybe she should get her sister to cover for her at the bakery and take a nice long vacation before she completely lost her mind. Reed might be interested now, but the day would come when he'd leave and return to Hollywood, and she'd be left with the fallout... again.

Zinnia crept along the hallway until she heard a muffled woman's voice, followed by a small sob. She froze, glancing around to see who was there. She didn't see anyone, but a door to the left was barely cracked opened.

"I can't... do this... anymore," a woman said, her voice hitching on her words. "It's too hard, Kat. I should've taken the other costume design job out in L.A. instead of this one."

"Shhh. Don't say that. It's going to be okay, babe. You just have to trust me."

The second voice was familiar and sounded an awful lot like Krissy's. Zinnia knew she should move on. The conversation was private, and she had no business eavesdropping. She turned to go, but her shoe got caught on the edge of a throw carpet, and she went down on one knee, barely managing to balance the cookies.

"You've been saying that for two years!" the other woman said, her voice now full of anger. "Why should I believe you this time?"

There was a heavy sigh and then Krissy said, "Because our breakup is about to become very public. And once that happens, we can be together."

Unable to get up without losing all the cookie boxes, Zinnia placed them on the ground and pushed herself to her feet. As she leaned down to get the boxes, the conversation continued.

"Right. Because after all these years of expecting you to marry for the family dynasty, your dad is really going to just accept that you're a lesbian and you're in love with a nobody from Nowhereville, Montana? Come on, Kat. You have your head in the clouds."

Lesbian? Kat—err Krissy was a lesbian?

"Holly—" Krissy started.

"Just go away," the other woman ordered. "I need time to think."

"But I—"

"I said go!" she shouted.

Zinnia got the cookies balanced in her arms and started back down the hall, but the door flew open and Krissy barreled out. The television star once again knocked right into Zinnia, sending her into the opposite wall as the cookies went flying.

"Oomph!" Zinnia cried out.

"What in the hell are you doing here?" Krissy demanded. Her face was set in a scowl, and her eyes flashed with anger.

Zinnia stared down at the crumpled boxes and wanted to scream. Roughly half of the cookies had tumbled out onto the floor, and she had no doubt the rest were ruined after the fall. She waved at the boxes. "I was delivering these to the parlor."

"This is the costume department. The parlor is on the *other side* of the house," Krissy said with a hiss. "Were you spying on me?"

"What?" Zinnia jerked back, rubbing at her shoulder. "No. Of course not. Why would I do that?"

"Oh, I don't know. Maybe because you're afraid Reed's lying to you about us?"

Zinnia definitely wasn't afraid of that. Especially not now that she had reason to believe Krissy played for the other team.

The door creaked open, and the most beautiful woman Zinnia had ever seen peeked out. She had wide dark eyes, alabaster skin, and shiny black hair. She was wearing skinny jeans and a satin blouse that hung off one shoulder. Everything about her was perfect except for her tear-stained cheeks. The woman placed a hand on Krissy's arm. "Kat, this isn't helping anything."

Krissy glanced at her, and in a very faint voice, she said, "Sorry." Then she shoved her hands in her pockets and stalked down the hallway.

"I'm sorry about that," Holly said. "She's having a bad day."

"I guess so," Zinnia said, kneeling to clean up the cookie mess. "Is she at least feeling better after her trip to the healer?"

Holly nodded as she helped Zinnia collect the wolf cookies. "The rash is mostly gone. By tomorrow, she should be as good as new."

"That's good." Zinnia clamped her mouth shut, not knowing what else to say.

"Zinnia, right?" Holly asked.

"Yeah." She shoveled the last of the broken cookies into a box.

"Listen, about Kat, I mean Krissy—" Holly started.

"Zinnia?" Reed's voice came from the end of the hallway. "What are you doing down here?"

She glanced back at him.

He was wearing sweats and a T-shirt and striding toward her, his hand outstretched. "What happened? Did you get lost?"

Zinnia stood and nodded. "I was having trouble finding the parlor and ended up surprising someone." She waved at the mess at her feet. "This is the end result of an unfortunate collision."

Holly rose gracefully. "Krissy was upset and didn't see her."

"Right," Reed said, his expression darkening. "I'm sure it was an accident, just like it was earlier today at the café."

Zinnia shook her head. "No, I think this time really was an accident. She didn't see me."

"Kat ran into her at the café?" The pain in Holly's dark eyes was unmistakable.

"She was just being obnoxious. I wouldn't read too much into it," Reed said, giving her a sympathetic smile.

"As usual." Holly smoothed her blouse and without another word she strode back into the nearby room.

Reed held his hand out to Zinnia. "Leave the cookies. We'll get one of the crew to clean them up."

"Oh, no." Zinnia took a step back. "I couldn't do that. Just point me to some cleaning supplies and I'll—"

"Hey, Paul, it's Reed," he said, talking into his phone. "Can you send someone from the cleaning crew down to the west corridor? We've had a cookie incident. Thanks." He winked at her and grabbed her hand. "Let's go. I have a scene to get ready for."

Zinnia opened her mouth to protest, but Reed was already ushering her down the hall, shaking his head.

"Nope. I'm not leaving you here and I'm about to be late for my call time. You're just gonna have to come with me, or Delaney is gonna lose her mind. You don't want to get me into trouble do you?"

She rolled her eyes but had to suppress a smile. The

boy she'd been best friends with thirteen years ago hadn't changed. Not one bit. He could still charm her into anything, and that thought sent a thrill straight to her toes.

DELANEY, the five-foot-eleven, redheaded goddess waved a hand at a canvas foldup chair and said, "You can watch from here."

"Thanks," Zinnia said, smiling at the gorgeous assistant director.

She stepped back and swept her gaze over Zinnia before narrowing her eyes at her. "This is a professional shoot. One peep out of you and you'll be shown out. Got it?"

Zinnia resented the woman's tone and had to bite back a snarky reply. She wasn't a damned groupie. Zinnia had only agreed to stay because Reed had asked her to. But instead of making waves, she just nodded and took her seat.

Delaney raised one skeptical eyebrow, but then someone across the set called her name, and she stalked off.

Reed, who'd left to get into wardrobe, appeared on set and strode over to her wearing a robe.

Zinnia swept her gaze over him. "I thought you were filming a dinner scene? Are you two engaging in a bedroom picnic or what?"

He winced. "Sorry. Change of plans. Now that the

healer worked her magic on Krissy's rash, we're doing the love scene… in a bathtub."

"Oh." Zinnia stood. "That's awkward, isn't it? I should probably go. Neither of you are going to want a perfect stranger watching you film that."

His hand slipped into hers and he held on gently, stopping her from running off the set. "I still want to see you after. Can I come by the shop? Will you be there?"

She shook her head. The day had been impossibly long, and while she should go back to the store to redo the cookies she'd dropped, she'd already decided she was going to bake them at home. She needed to relax and put her feet up. Have a glass—or bottle—of wine while watching mindless television. "I'm going home. If you get done at a reasonable hour you can meet me there."

"Done." He had her scribble her address down on the back of a napkin. After stuffing it into his pocket, he leaned down and brushed his lips over her cheek. "I'll be there as soon as I can."

She stared up into his impossibly blue eyes and couldn't help the small sigh that escaped her lips.

"What was that about?" he asked, his gaze searching hers.

Zinnia gave him a small smile and lightly patted his chest. "Just wondering how long it's going to be before you break my heart again." He opened his mouth to say something, but Zinnia pressed her fingers to his lips and said, "Shhh. We both know you're going to leave eventually. I'm just being realistic about it. Now go work. I'll see you later tonight."

She left him standing there as her heart raced. Had she really said that? She glanced over her shoulder to find him still staring after her. A giggle bubbled up from the back of her throat when she realized she'd left him speechless. Finally, she'd been the one to leave him off balance instead of the other way around. *Good,* she thought. It was about time the tables were turned for once.

Navigating the large house wasn't any easier as she tried to make her way back toward the front door. The crew was filming on the third floor, and when she descended the first set of stairs, she found herself in an unfamiliar, unlit hallway. This hadn't been the way Reed had led her to the set earlier. She gritted her teeth and ran her hand along the wall, looking for a light switch. She didn't find one, but instead of turning around and embarrassing herself in front of Reed, she headed toward the faint light at the end of the hallway.

The sound of voices was music to her ears, indicating she was either headed toward the main hallway or she could at least get directions. She sped up as the voices started to fade and rushed around the corner.

Two women were half hidden in the shadows off to the left of the grand staircase, two women she recognized. And when they bent their heads together, their lips touching in a gentle kiss, Zinnia froze.

Krissy and Holly kissed softly, then Krissy wrapped

her arms around the other woman, and the kiss turned heated.

Zinnia took a step back, not wanting to get accused of spying again, but she needn't have bothered. Krissy was so focused on Holly, she didn't seem to notice anything else around her.

"I'm so sorry, babe," Krissy said. "Can you forgive me?"

Holly let out a deep sigh. "It's not about forgiveness, Kat. You know I can't keep doing this. I don't want to hide who I am or what we have."

Krissy bit down on her bottom lip as she stared into Holly's eyes. "You know I can't just come out. The show, the publicity—"

"Your father," Holly finished for her.

"Yes, my father," Krissy said, heatedly. "I can't just defy him. You don't understand."

"Oh, I understand perfectly, Kat," Holly said very quietly. "His approval and bank account mean more to you than I do."

Krissy took a step back. "That's not fair."

"Maybe not, but it's the truth." Holly stepped up close to the actress, tucked a lock of her blond hair behind her ear then strode off down the stairs with Krissy watching her as she went.

When Holly's footsteps faded into silence, Krissy let out a sigh and turned toward the hallway where Zinnia was still standing.

Oh, shit! Zinnia stepped back into the hallway, collected herself, then strode back around the corner, acting as if she hadn't seen or heard anything. "Krissy, hey, fancy meeting you here," she said with a nervous smile. "I was just on my way out. I think Reed and the crew might be waiting for you."

Krissy let out a noncommittal grunt and brushed past Zinnia without a word.

Zinnia glanced over her shoulder at her. Krissy's shoulders were slumped, and she was shaking her head, clearly lost in her own thoughts, no doubt about her conversation with Holly. Zinnia felt a little sorry for Krissy. She knew it must be awful to be in love with someone and have to hide their relationship.

But what Zinnia didn't understand was why Krissy acted so put out about Reed spending time with another woman if she was in love with Holly. Was it just their image she was worried about? Did she think the ratings would go down if the public learned they weren't really a couple? Perhaps. She made a mental note to ask Reed about it later. In the meantime, she had cookies to bake, and she needed to prepare for an evening with the television star. A slow smile claimed her lips as she floated down the second set of stairs and out of the front door of the gorgeous Victorian.

CHAPTER 6

Reed lowered himself into the claw foot tub and watched as Krissy slipped out of her robe. She was wearing a nude-colored bathing suit, and her blond hair had been pinned to the top of her head. The rash was gone, leaving her skin once again lightly tanned and flawless.

His costar was gorgeous, and there was a time in his life when he'd considered dating her. It certainly would've made things easier if they'd been attracted to each other. But while Krissy was a giant flirt, when he flirted back that spark in her eye that drew so many of her fans to her always faded away. He didn't know why, but when they were alone together with no cameras rolling, that chemistry between them fizzled out like a wet firecracker. It was just as well. He had no interest in her now, and if they'd ever slept together, it would've just been a huge mistake.

"Okay, Krissy. Sit between Reed's legs and lean back

into him, your head tilted up so you can gaze lovingly at your fiancé," Delaney said.

"Do we have to do this tonight?" Krissy asked. "I thought the schedule had been rearranged for a fight scene." Her fists were clenched, and her brows were pinched in what looked to be frustration.

"Your rash is gone, right?" Delaney asked in a sharp tone.

"Yes. So? I got all geared up for a fight, not a love scene." Krissy glanced at Reed and made a face.

Reed just raised his eyebrows. Something was wrong. It wasn't like Krissy to argue with the directors.

"Plans changed," Delaney said coldly, clearly not in the mood to take any shit. "If you hadn't been playing in the woods earlier today, we'd have already gotten this scene and been home by now. Get in. I've already had a fourteen-hour day."

Krissy sucked in a sharp breath, and Reed could almost see her swallowing her anger.

"What wrong?" he whispered once she was in the tub and leaning against his chest.

"Nothing. Forget it." She was tense. Every muscle was coiled as if she was ready to bound right out of the tub given half a chance.

"Hey," he said, rubbing her shoulders lightly. "Let's both try to relax so we can get through this and call it a night, huh?"

She tilted her head to the side, giving him better access to her neck, and said, "Yeah. Okay."

"That's good," Delaney said. "The small smiles, the tenderness, this is a great opener for this scene."

Krissy tensed again, and Reed noticed her lips thin into a grimace.

"Krissy!" Delaney admonished. "What are you doing?"

"Sorry," she mumbled and glanced back at Reed with weary eyes. "I'm really not in the right frame of mind for this."

He wasn't either if he was honest. All he could think about was tearing out of there and heading off to Zinnia's place. All he wanted to do was wrap her in his arms and kiss her again. Having Krissy in his arms seemed like a betrayal, even though he was only doing his job. But if he let his reluctance get the better of him, they'd be there filming all night, and that was the last thing he was going to let happen.

"You can do this," he whispered into her ear. "Just imagine the person you really would rather be with. Picture him in your mind and pretend he's the one running his hands over your soft skin."

She let out a small huff of laughter. "Yeah, sure. If only *he* were here right now instead of you."

He didn't miss the sarcasm in her voice but chose to ignore it as he ran his thumb from the base of her skull down her neck. "Imagine him kissing you here," he whispered as he leaned in and lightly brushed his lips over her pulse. He knew then that she really had no interest in him. Her skin was cool, and her pulse was a steady beat. Having his hands and lips on her hadn't caused one physical response. He couldn't help but wonder what the scene at the hot springs was about. Why had she followed him there and acted jealous?

"That's it," Delaney said. "Good work, Reed. Krissy, reach back and place your hand on his cheek."

Krissy did what she was told.

Then Delaney made them run through the scene again three more times before she told Krissy to turn and wrap her arms and legs around Reed.

Once she was in position, they were both stiff and awkward. Reed reached up, intending to smooth her hair back, but he missed and awkwardly poked her in the eye.

"Ouch!" She jerked back, covering the side of her face with her hand. "What was that for?"

"Sorry," he said sheepishly. "I'm just… I can't relax."

"That didn't help." She removed her hand and blinked a few times. Her eye was watery and red.

"Hold on." The makeup artist ran in and administered some eye drops then touched up Krissy's makeup.

Delaney yelled, "Action!"

Reed stared down at her intently, trying to think of all the things he was supposed to want to do with her. Instead a chill washed over him, and his skin felt tight, like he needed a hot shower to wash away the uncomfortable feeling of having Krissy wrapped around him. She didn't look any more comfortable than he did. They both awkwardly moved through the scene five times before Delaney yelled, "Cut!"

The assistant director stalked over to them and leaned down. Her voice was low but full of disdain. "I don't know what's going on between you two, but you'd better snap out of it. If you don't, I'm going to put a goddamned porno movie on and make you watch it until you're ready to ride each other like fucking rock stars. Got it?"

Krissy rolled her eyes. "You wouldn't do that."

"Won't I? I have a date tonight, and if you two make me late, heads will roll. Now figure out how to get hot for each other, or I'll figure it out for you."

Reed watched her go as a production assistant arrived and added more bubbles to the water. Once he retreated, Reed closed his eyes and imagined Zinnia as she'd been in the hot spring earlier that day. His body instantly heated. Every part of him was hard and ready for her, and his fingers ached to touch her, to tease every inch of her soft body as he explored all of her secret places.

He heard Delaney's faint voice across the room and knew they'd started to film again, but he was too busy picturing himself tasting Zinnia's nipple.

"Now, Reed. Show her how much you want her," Delaney whispered from behind him.

He opened his eyes and knew that Krissy was still wrapped around him, but his mind had gone to a completely new place as he reached for her. He didn't see the gorgeous blond actress. All he saw in his mind was Zinnia's flushed face after he'd all but devoured her in the spring earlier that day.

He brought his hand up, caressed her cheek and then pulled her in tight, his lips possessing hers. He felt her go pliant in his arms, surrendering herself to him, and then suddenly a loud voice yelled, "Cut!"

Krissy quickly pulled back, pressing the back of her hand to her mouth. "What the fuck was that?"

"That was onscreen magic, darling," Delaney said, beaming at them. "Nice job, Reed. You even had me believing you couldn't wait to nail her." She turned and looked at the filming crew. "It's a wrap, people. Go home. Get some rest and sleep in tomorrow, but we'll be filming in the afternoon. The rest of you, make sure you're here with enough time for makeup and wardrobe."

Krissy scrambled out of the tub and quickly wrapped herself in the robe one of the production assistants was holding out for her. Reed watched her run off the set and wondered what he'd done to cross the line.

But deep down he knew. He'd tapped into too much emotion. Emotions that had nothing to do with her or the characters they were playing. Emotions she'd know damned well were for someone else. And no matter how much they told themselves it was their job to act, no one ever wanted to feel like they were a stand-in for someone else. And that's exactly what she'd just become.

Reed hauled himself out of the tub, feeling like the world's largest ass, and followed her.

He knocked once and said, "Krissy? Are you all right?"

The door swung open, and she just stood there, staring at his chest. Then she raised her gaze and in a breezy voice said, "Sure. Why wouldn't I be?"

He glanced back toward the set. "What happened back there... I'm sorry if I took it too far."

She shrugged. "Delaney's happy."

"I know, but—"

"Forget it, Reed," she said softly. "It's just a scene. You did your job and I did mine. Now go find that girl and get her out of your system. You won't be satisfied until you do."

He knew Zinnia would never be out of his system. It'd been thirteen years, and he wanted her just as much as he had then—more now that they'd shared the day in the hot spring. But instead of contradicting her, he just nodded and went to find the one girl he'd never been able to forget.

REED KNOCKED on the door of the ivy-covered cottage and smiled. The place had gingerbread trim along the front porch and fit Zinnia perfectly. He could just imagine her bustling around in her kitchen with the scent of warm chocolate fudge cookies in the air. The image stirred a longing inside of him he hadn't felt in thirteen years.

The door was flung open, and there she was. Her

flushed cheeks and plump red lips pulled a barely audible groan from him as he stepped into her, wrapping one arm around her waist.

"Well, hello to you, too," she said, smiling up at him.

"Please tell me you're not right in the middle of something important that can't wait a few minutes."

"Why?" she asked, giving him an amused look of suspicion.

"Because I've been waiting all night to do this." He took her by the hand, pulled her out onto the porch, and then bent his head and brushed his lips over hers. She instantly melted into him, and it was all he could do to stop himself from walking her backward into her house, slamming the door, and taking her right there.

Back when they'd known each other as teens, they'd never held hands, never kissed, never done more than share a slow dance at a high school homecoming. But he'd remembered the curve of her body in his arms then, and she was even better now. All soft and pliant and female. He couldn't remember when he'd felt so out of control around a woman.

Her hand curled around a swath of his cotton shirt and he opened his mouth, his tongue finding hers and tasting her again. Chocolate and sugar and spice. She reminded him of Christmas and was a package he couldn't wait to unwrap. Without a word, he lifted her up and set her on the porch railing, shifting to move between her legs. Then he dipped his head again, covering her mouth and kissing her deeply, claiming her as his.

Something stirred deep inside of him. Something primal and raw and sacred. His skin tingled and heated just as it always did at the beginning of his shift, but that pull in his gut that would force him into a werewolf was missing. He wasn't going to turn—not now at least—but his wolf was there right beneath the surface, letting Reed know *this was the one.*

His hold on her tightened, but he broke the kiss and just stared down at her sweet face, shock rolling through him in waves. Reed had known for years that he'd wanted her, that he'd had an insane crush on her and deeply regretted never asking her out. But what he hadn't known is that his inner wolf had craved her. That was obvious now, and for the first time in his life, he could feel his wolf starting to take over.

The urge to bite her, to bind her to him forever, was right there at the surface.

He pulled back but couldn't bring himself to let her go as he sucked in a deep breath, trying to steady himself. It didn't take long for his wolf to settle, much to his relief. Knowing he could control himself meant he could stay. If he couldn't, he'd have had to leave. There was one thing he'd never do—bite a woman without her consent. Wolves who claimed their mates without explicit consent were complete trash in his opinion. He wanted a partner, not someone magically bound to him who didn't want to be there.

"Reed?" she asked softly, searching his face.

"Yes?" He trailed his fingers up and down her spine, unable to stop touching her.

"My cookies are going to burn."

He dipped his head again and pressed soft, lingering kisses on her neck. "Do you care?"

She tilted her head to the side as she breathed, "No, I guess not."

He smiled against her skin and dropped his other hand down to cup her round ass.

"Oh, god," she said, her breath warm against his ear.

The wind picked up, and then a loud rumble of thunder came out of nowhere, making the house shake.

"Holy balls!" Zinnia jerked against him as the skies opened up and dumped sheets of rain on Witch Island. Even though the small porch was covered, the wind caused the rain to come in sideways, pelting them both.

Reed pulled her off the railing and turned around, instantly shielding her from the massive storm.

"Get inside!" she cried and yanked him into her warm house.

Reed stood in her entryway, his back side soaked to the bone. "Christ, Zinnia. Does that happen often here?"

She pushed her wet hair out of her face. "Often enough I guess. Being on an island, the storms can be intense." She took him by the hand. "Come on. Let's get you out of those wet clothes."

The words hung in the air for just a moment before she gave him a slow, wicked smile and said, "This time I'm going to watch."

CHAPTER 7

Zinnia's heart raced and thundered against her ribcage. Had she really just implied she was going to watch him get naked? Judging by the heated expression on Reed's face, the answer was a resounding yes.

"You first," he said, his voice raspy with pure lust.

Oh boy. She needed to be more careful of what she let slip out of her mouth around him. Or did she?

He grabbed her by the hand and pulled her through the small cottage toward the hallway off her living room. "Which one is your bedroom?"

She cleared her throat. "The one at the end of the hall."

His pace quickened and in no time, he ushered her through her large master bedroom and into the en suite bathroom. Once they were standing in front of the shower, he let her go and took two steps back. After sweeping his gaze down her body, he met her eyes and said, "Are you sure you want to do this, Zinnia?"

Was she sure? She glanced at the walk-in shower and almost laughed. How many times had she imagined this scene over the years? Granted he'd never been soaked from head to toe, but then neither had she. Zinnia nodded and slowly untied the apron. After she tossed it over the side of the tub, she raised one eyebrow at him. "Your turn."

His lips stretched into a slow seductive smile. "So, this is how it's going to be? We'll take turns?"

She nodded. "Yep. And whoever ends up naked first gets to finish undressing the other one."

He laughed as he reached behind him and yanked his long-sleeved thermal over his head. Tossing it next to her apron he asked, "Are you making the rules up as you go along, Franklyn?"

She just stared at his pecs and broad shoulders and tried not to lick her lips. Good goddess, he was gorgeous. It had only been a few hours since she'd seen him without his shirt on, but somehow he looked even more spectacular than he had at the hot spring. Maybe it was the lighting. Or the fact that he was in her house, standing in front of her shower. Or perhaps it was because now that she'd had a taste of him, every single one of her nerves were on fire.

Unable to resist, Zinnia took a step forward and placed her hands on his chest. A visible shiver ran through him and she glanced up into his deep blue eyes and asked, "Are my hands cold?"

He shook his head. "Not even a little bit."

"Oh." She gave him a pleased smile and ran her fingertips over his defined muscles, aching to kiss every inch of him. But when she moved in to do just that, he gently placed his hands on her shoulders and took a step back.

"Not yet, Zin. It's your turn, remember?" He stared pointedly at her chest and then raised one eyebrow.

She chuckled. "In a hurry, aren't you?"

"You're the one who can't keep her hands to herself."

"Touché." She grinned as she lifted one foot and pulled off the boot she'd been wearing. After placing it next to the tub, she freed her other foot and stood with her hands on her hips, waiting.

He kicked off his shoes, and they went back and forth, removing socks, belts, and watches.

Finally, it was Zinnia's turn to strip out of her shirt. But she'd grown impatient of the game and was desperate to feel his warm skin against hers. Instead of stopping at her shirt, she stepped out of her jeans and then went for her bra.

"Wait," Reed said, placing his hands on her arms, stopping her. "Let me."

"Game over?" she asked, running her hands from his chest to his stomach.

"Over? Not even close, gorgeous. We're just getting started." He reached into the shower and turned the water on, and as the bathroom slowly started to fill with steam, he unlatched her bra. His fingers barely brushed over her skin as he ran them down her arms, taking the straps of her bra with them. Unable to wait a second longer, he filled his palms with her breasts and stared down at her, his breathing suddenly uneven. "Christ, you're spectacular."

Zinnia could've stood there forever in a state of bliss letting him run the pads of his thumbs over her nipples, but when he lowered his head and scraped his teeth over the sensitive peak, white hot desire sizzled at her core. She let out a gasp and instantly reached for the button of his jeans.

"Not yet, Zin," he said, shifting away from her touch. "You have to let me enjoy you first."

She was torn. Her hands were greedy to be touching him, but her body was begging for everything he had to offer. Her body won when his tongue laved at her nipple while his hands slid down to her hips and down further to her thighs, taking her white lace panties with him. She felt the cloth fall to her feet as his hands moved back up. One rested on her hip while the other moved between her legs, softly probing at her warm center.

"Fuck me, Zin. You're so hot, so ready," he mumbled as he moved his mouth to her other breast, giving her other nipple some much needed attention.

"I would," she said breathlessly, "but you won't let me get you out of your pants."

He froze. Then, as if she'd said the magic words, he straightened and placed both of her hands on the waistband of his jeans. "Playtime's over, princess."

She gave him a self-satisfied smile as she worked his jeans over and pushed them and his boxer briefs down his thighs. "That's what you think, television star."

"Oh? And what is—oh fuck."

Zinnia had already dropped to her knees and took his hard, velvety cock in her hand. She was gazing up at him when she wrapped her lips around him and tasted his tip. His body trembled with the effort to stay still, and when she took him fully, letting his length hit the back of her throat, he groaned.

"Dammit, Zin. Jesus fucking Christ, you're going to kill me."

Killing him wasn't in the plan, but she most certainly intended to make him lose his mind. Zinnia slipped her hand down to the base of his cock and started stroking him while she moved her head back and forth, sucking, tasting, and teasing.

"Zin," he groaned, burying his hand in her hair, his hips rocking ever so slightly as he barely held himself in check.

She glanced up at him, pleased to see the mixture of ecstasy and sheer torture on his beautiful face. He seemed to sense she was watching him and glanced down, their gazes meeting. His eyes were wild with need, and the moment was so fucking hot that Zinnia thought she'd melt right there in front of him.

Keeping her eyes locked on his, she ever so slowly released him from her mouth and then ran her tongue from his base to the tip.

Reed froze. Loving the effect she was having on

him, she wrapped her lips around him again. But before she could do anything else, he reached down and pulled her up and into the shower. He spun her around, pressing his chest to her back, his hands everywhere, on her breasts, her hips, her thighs, and he shoved his hand between her legs, cupping her while kneading one breast and sucking hard on her neck.

Zinnia was so consumed by his touch, she barely felt the water sluicing over their bodies. The only thing she could focus on was his thumb as he slowly worked it ever so closer to—

"Oh!" she gasped when he found the bundle of nerves that made her blood hum with pure pleasure.

"I'm gonna need you to come fast and hard for me, Zin," he growled against her neck as he increased the pressure. "Because I'm losing my fucking mind right now, baby, and once I'm inside you, I'm not going to be able to wait."

His words created an inferno deep in her core and when he slipped not one, but two fingers inside of her while still keeping the pressure with his thumb, her entire body started to tremble.

"That's it, baby. Let it all go," he said as he pinched her nipple hard and thrust his fingers deeper. "Come for me, now."

His words were like a lightning rod, pulling her orgasm from her, the pleasure crashing through her as her insides throbbed with an intensity she'd never experienced before.

"Reed," she cried. "Yes. Oh, god, yes." Throwing her

head back against his shoulder, she held onto his neck as he continued to work her sex until the first orgasm rolled into the second and then the third. All she could do was hold on and let him pleasure her until she was limp in his arms.

"That was... incredible," she said and turned her head toward him to place a soft kiss on his stubbled jaw.

"No, you're the incredible one," he said, his voice raw with pure lust.

Just the sound of his need was enough to fortify her weakened body, and she started to turn into him, already reaching for his throbbing cock. When her hand wrapped around him, he let out a hiss and said, "I'm on the edge, love. If you do anything close to what you did last time, I'm not going to be able to hold back."

She smiled, completely satisfied by the effect she had on him. "Would you rather be inside me?"

"Yes," he said through clenched teeth.

"Okay." Zinnia released him, turned around, and bent over as she pressed her hands against the cool tile.

"Holy shit, Zin," he whispered as he grabbed her hip with one of his hands and ran the other down her spine. "You're fucking gorgeous, you know that?"

"Not as gorgeous as you are," she said, rocking her hips back into him.

His hard cock pressed against her, and she closed her eyes in anticipation, quivering with pure need. How many times had she imagined them together like this? Hundreds. She'd dreamed about him, fantasized what it might be like to finally have him filling her. In every one of those fantasies, she'd imagined them in a bed, usually missionary position, with both of them staring lovingly into each other's eyes.

Never had she imagined that if given the chance to be with Reed, she would find herself bent over in the shower waiting for him to fuck her from behind. But now that she was here, she wouldn't change a thing. Not even for all the money in the world. She'd never been more turned on in her entire life and had never come so hard, so easily, or been so consumed by anyone.

She already knew that her night with Reed was going to be the best sex of her life, and it had nothing to do with romance or their past friendship. What they had was pure, off-the-charts chemistry.

"Reed?" she said, breathless.

"Yes?" he replied, grinding his hips into her, letting the length of him slide over her slick heat.

"I need you inside of me. Now."

He let out a low chuckle and continued to work himself against her flesh as he said, "Soon, love. Soon." His movements were slow, deliberate, and downright delicious as the fire inside of her only continued to build. Her breath came quicker, and she rocked against him, needing to feel more of him and yet reveling in his torturous movements. "Be right back," he whispered in her ear.

She was about to protest when she heard the faint

rustle of what must've been a foil package, and she wondered where he'd managed to find a condom.

But all thoughts flew out of her head when he wrapped one arm around her waist, pressed his hand to her flat stomach, and reached once again between her legs and found her most sensitive spot. And just as she let out a gasp of pleasure, he drove into her from behind, burying himself deep.

"Holy fuck," she muttered as her eyes rolled into the back of her head.

"Are you okay?" he asked, holding completely still.

"More than okay. Much more." She hung her head and pressed her ass back, wanting to take him even deeper.

"Thank god," he said on a groan and started to move.

Between his cock filling her and his finger rolling over that perfect bundle of nerves, it didn't take long for that familiar pressure to build. That perfect ache of pleasure was right there, pushing her to the edge as he thrust into her over and over and over again, harder and harder as his breathing became ragged and out of control.

"More, Reed," she demanded, jerking her hips back to meet him. "More. Just like that. Yes! Just. Like. That."

One hand tightened around her hip as he managed to hold her completely still, ravaging her with his long, hard thrusts while torturing her sex with his fingers. And when she couldn't take it one second more, she reached down and pressed his finger to her throbbing clit and tumbled with a spectacular cry of ecstasy into another orgasm that shuddered through her entire body.

"Zinnia," she heard Reed call out as he thrust one last time and spilled into her, shuddering with his own release.

It was as if the world had blinked out and then reappeared in technicolor, Zinnia thought as she found herself pressed up against the tile wall, her wolf still holding her from behind. Her blue and silver tiles seemed brighter while the white walls illuminated the room. She twisted her head and smiled up into Reed's deep blue eyes. "Well. That was certainly a nice way to say hello."

He chuckled and tucked a lock of her wet hair behind her ear. "That was fucking insane."

"Wanna do it again?"

His eyes widened. "Right now?"

A small giggle escaped her lips as she shook her head. "I can barely hold myself up. Maybe after we—oh shit! The cookies!" Zinnia pulled away from him, hopped out of the shower, grabbed a towel hanging on the back of the door, and raced into her kitchen.

Smoke was curling out of the oven, and when she pulled the door open, the piercing sound of the smoke alarm went off, making her wince. "Shit, shit, shit!"

"Take care of the alarm. I'll deal with the oven," Reed called. He was standing right behind her, completely naked, and dripping water all over her floor.

She blinked and yelled, "Do you want a robe or something?"

He shook his head, already reaching to turn the oven off. Leaning into her, he said, "I'm fine. Get the alarm before we both suffer from hearing damage."

"Right." She tightened the towel around her body and hurried to her pantry where she kept her kitchen stepladder. After stationing it under the smoke detector, she climbed up and hit the reset button.

Nothing happened.

She pressed it again.

Nothing.

"Dammit! Shut up!" she cried as she reached up and ripped the plastic housing right off the ceiling. In the process, she managed to lose her grip and the entire alarm flew to the floor. Little plastic pieces scattered, the battery rolled out, and most importantly, the obnoxious noise ceased. She let out a sigh of relief. "Thank the gods."

"I think the cookies are dead," Reed said.

Zinnia squinted through the smoke still concentrated in her kitchen and winced. "Oops. I guess I got a little distracted."

"A little?" He chuckled as he opened the window.

A rush of cold air whooshed in along with the sound of the thundering rain. In no time the smoke vanished, but rain was pouring in through the window, soaking her counter and floor.

"Damn, that's one nasty storm," Reed said closing the window.

Zinnia shivered. She'd lost her towel somewhere along the way and wrapped her arms around herself as she stared at Reed's sculpted body. Goddamn, he was beautiful.

"Zin?" There was humor in his tone as he stalked back over to her. "You look like a woman who might be hungry for something other than cookies."

She reached up and pressed her hand to his scruffy cheek. "I guess I wasn't quite as satiated as I thought."

He turned his head and kissed the inside of her palm. "You have no idea how glad I am to hear you say that." Then he scooped her up into his arms and hauled her back into her bedroom. But this time as he settled beside her on her bed, instead of the almost out-of-control wolf he'd been in the bathroom, his movements were slow and deliberate as he took his time getting to know every inch of her.

They were silent, communicating only with soft kisses and caresses, each of their bodies responding to the other as if they'd danced this waltz before, and Zinnia knew then that she'd never feel as attuned with another person as she did with Reed. And when an image of him leaving town to go back to his life in Los Angeles flashed in her mind, she firmly pushed it away. Nothing was going to ruin this moment with him. Whatever time she had with him was a gift, and she wasn't going to ruin it.

"I could stay right here with you forever, Zin," Reed said softly as if reading her thoughts, rolling them both over so that he was positioned above her, his intense gaze locked on hers.

"If this storm keeps up, you might just get your wish." She pressed two fingers to his lips and smiled up at him when he kissed them with such tenderness that it almost made her heart break.

He took both of her hands, laced his fingers through hers, and then pressed them against the bed over her head. Staring down at her with tenderness and raw emotion swimming in his expression he said, "This night with you means everything to me. I don't think you'll ever understand just how much I missed you."

Her breath left her as tears stung her eyes. She did understand. She'd missed him with everything she had, but she'd done her best to bury her longing. Now that he was looking down at her with something that looked suspiciously like love in his eyes, she couldn't hold back anymore. "You're the only one I've ever wanted. Make love to me."

He let out a barely audible, guttural sound that seemed to come from deep in his gut, and then he kissed her, slowly, deeply, passionately and didn't stop until he'd made good on her demand.

CHAPTER 8

R eed stirred from a contented sleep, already reaching for Zinnia. He curled into her, spooning her from behind with his arm wrapped around her waist. She was warm and soft, and her hair still smelled like sugar and spice. The longing that he'd carried for her since he was sixteen years old came roaring back, and it was all he could do to keep from waking her up and taking her all over again.

Their first encounter in the shower had been a culmination of years of frustration. He'd been out of his mind with desire for her and had caved to most of his baser instincts. He'd needed her, needed to make her his in every way possible. By some miracle he'd managed to keep himself from biting her, but it'd been hard. Real fucking hard. But that had been his wolf talking. He'd known that and had kept that side of him at bay,

Then he'd made love to her. The man he'd become

had poured every ounce of emotion he possessed into showing her just how much he cared, and by the time he'd entered her, he'd known. He'd never walk away from her again. He couldn't. Wouldn't. She was his other half, something he hadn't understood when they'd still been teenagers.

The morning couldn't have been more perfect with the storm still brewing, the rain pelting relentlessly against the windows, and the woman of his dreams still wrapped in his arms. He could stay there forever if it weren't for the show. But unfortunately, he had to get to the set... eventually. Reed tightened his hold on her, felt himself get hard again, and rained a trail of kisses down her neck.

"Good morning," she said sleepily.

"Morning, gorgeous. How'd you sleep?"

"Great. Someone wore me out." She twisted just enough to plant a soft kiss on his lips.

"Someone would be happy to do it all over again." He ran his hand up her side, letting his fingers trail over the side of her bare breast.

"That could probably be arranged."

He chuckled softly and suddenly remembered a night long ago when they'd lain in almost exactly the same position, only they'd both been fully clothed and the prospect of sex hadn't even been close to being on the table. "Do you remember that one night we spent watching movies at your house cuddled up on the couch?"

She sucked in a small breath. "You mean the night

Laura Whatshername bailed on you just a week after your brother…" Zin shook her head. "I never could understand how someone could be so selfish."

He waited for the stone-cold rage to slip into his psyche just as it always did when he was reminded of the night his older brother had been shot and killed in a neighborhood convenience store robbery. Reese had been on his way home from work when he'd stopped in for some butter his mom had asked him to pick up. As he was paying, the robber shot both him and the cashier and ran off with all of two hundred and three dollars. The three-time offender had been caught two hours later and was still in prison.

Reed's life had shattered apart. His mother had a breakdown, and his father was so consumed with his political interests that Reed had pretty much been on his own. Laura, who he'd been dating for two months, told him she hadn't signed up to be a grief counselor and bailed.

Zinnia had been the only one who'd been there for him. He'd arrived at her house with a bottle of tequila, ready to drown his pain in the bottle of José. But Zinnia had gently taken the booze from him and led him down to the basement. She told him they were going to lose themselves in junk food and whatever movies they could find in her mom's vast collection. They'd watched everything from American Pie to Die Hard, and it had been the first night since he'd lost his brother that he hadn't woken up wishing he'd died, too. Zinnia had let him hold her, no questions asked. There wasn't any need for clarification on their relationship. No expectations. Nothing but friendship and a sense that she just knew he needed someone and needed to do something normal.

Not that cuddling with her had been normal for them, but the junk food and movies were. They'd fallen asleep spooning on the couch and had woken up in the same position.

"I almost kissed you that morning when we both woke up. Did you know that?" he asked her.

"What?" she asked, glancing at him over her shoulder. "You did not. That had to be the furthest thing from your mind. Besides, we both had morning garlic fry breath." She wrinkled her nose and covered her mouth. "Can you imagine how bad that would've been?"

He just laughed. "Zinnia, I was sixteen and had just woken up with a hot girl in my arms. Do you really think my mind was capable of processing anything besides how good you felt?"

"I wasn't hot," she mumbled.

"The hell you weren't. The only thing that stopped me was the fact that your mom suddenly arrived with waffles and orange juice, acting like it was no big deal that we'd just slept together."

"We didn't *sleep* together. We just happened to fall asleep while watching a movie. Besides, she knew we were just friends, and she felt bad about what you were going through."

"If she'd been five minutes later, we wouldn't have

just been friends anymore. Not if I'd had anything to say about it."

"You seem awfully sure of yourself," she said with a laugh. "What if I hadn't been into you?"

"Were you?" he asked, his tone sounding deadly serious even to his own ears.

Silence hung in the air.

"Zin?" he asked quietly. "It's okay if you weren't."

She let out a small huff of laughter as she shook her head. "That's not... Reed, I had the biggest crush on you back then. I just can't believe you didn't know it."

Pleasure filled him, and he was surprised by how much her answer pleased him. After placing a soft kiss below her ear, he asked, "How could I have known that? You were always the one going on about how we were just friends, and anytime I even hinted at being more, you shut me down and usually ended by calling me a jackass."

"That's because I always thought you were joking," she said. "And if I let myself believe there was any truth to your jokes, I was afraid my heart would be stomped on while you moved on to the class president or a cheerleader or that gorgeous, brunette girl who got a volleyball scholarship to UCLA."

The images of the three girls she referenced resurfaced in his memory. He hadn't thought about any of them in a long time. None of them had ever occupied his thoughts the way she had. But he thought they were attractive back in high school. "Yeah, they were pretty, and I won't deny they certainly caught my eye, but I want to make it clear that if I'd had you as my girlfriend, none of them would've had a chance. You were always the one I wanted." He rubbed his jaw in thought. "What was the volleyball player's name? The one who got a scholarship? I can't even remember."

Zinnia flipped around and glared at him. "You forgot Carly's name? Christ, Reed. You dated her a few months after she arrived in southern California. Do you just forget everyone who was ever important to you?"

He blinked. "What? I never dated Carly."

"Oh, come on." Zinnia rolled her eyes. "You two were in the tabloids, and when she came home for Christmas, she told us all about the fabulous parties you used to take her to."

"You're kidding me, right?" His jaw tightened, and he shook his head, disgusted. Why did everyone always manage to disappoint him? And why the fuck couldn't anyone ever just see him for the man he was and not some celebrity that could be used for status or furthering their career, or hell, even just bragging rights? "I saw her once out in L.A. after running into her at a diner at two in the morning. I think I gave her the address where an industry party was happening that same weekend, but I ended up not going and never saw her again."

"Seriously?" she asked. "You didn't introduce her to Harry Highlander, the werewolf who'd just won an Oscar?"

"No. Besides, that guy is a complete ass, and he's the last person I'd introduce to a friend of mine."

Zinnia frowned. "Damn. I can't believe she lied to us."

He sighed. "I can. It happens all the time. People have a strange view of celebrity. Everyone wants a piece of you for their own gain." Reed glanced down at her, his expression slightly puzzled. "Everyone except for you, that is."

She tilted her head to the side, gazing up at him curiously. "What makes you say that? How do you know I haven't already called the paparazzi and alerted them that you spent the night in my bed?"

He rolled his eyes. Besides the fact that he'd been with her every moment since he'd walked through her door, he already knew in his gut the very last thing she'd do was call in the paparazzi. She'd never been one for the spotlight. The last thing she'd want was for them to show up on her front doorstep. "Because I know you. And if you cared one bit about that crap, you'd have answered the postcards I sent you back then. Since you didn't, I just assumed you were unimpressed by my new life."

Her mouth fell open as she stared at him. "What did you say?"

"That you aren't impressed by stardom?" he asked, wondering why she was so surprised by that statement. "It's obvious, isn't it? If you were like the rest of them, you'd have written me back and—"

"Reed, I *did* write you back. Three long letters," she

said, averting her gaze as if she couldn't quite manage to look him in the eye. "You're the one who stopped communicating with me. I thought you just didn't have time for me anymore. But it was never because you landed the television show. I just missed you… missed us."

"You wrote me?" His voice was cold and distant even to his own ears. He'd never gotten her letters. Not even one. Was she lying, or had someone kept them from him?

She didn't say anything as she bit down on her bottom lip and stared over his shoulder at the window.

"Zinnia? Answer me. You wrote me? When?"

"I already told you," she shot back as she suddenly sat up, her face red with anger now. "After I got your post cards. Maybe a few days after each one."

He scrambled to sit up and face her. Everything in him screamed to take her back in his arms, but he needed more answers. Needed to understand what exactly had happened back then. If she had written him, that meant he'd spent the last thirteen years obsessing about why his best friend had vanished out of his life. "Where? Do you remember where you sent them?"

She shrugged. "Does it matter now? I think I sent them to the return address. It was some house in Beverly Hills. That's all I remember."

"Shit!" He ran a hand over his face. Then he hung his head. "You wrote me back." His words were a statement, not a question.

"Yeah, so? Then I never heard from you again." She pushed the covers back and swung her feet out of the bed.

But Reed reached out and grabbed her hand, pulling her back to him. "You didn't just blow me off." He was smiling now, all of his empty places full of love for her. She'd been his then, and she was his now. There was no way he was letting her go. Not yet, not until she understood.

"No. Like I said—" she started.

"I know," he said gently. "In your mind, I'm the one who ditched you. But don't you understand, Zin? I never got your letters. I thought you were pissed that I left or something. I didn't know you'd written. If I had, I'd have never stopped writing you."

"You never got my letters?" She blinked. "How is that possible? They never came back to me."

He shrugged. "No real idea other than it's possible they were tossed in with the rest of the fan mail. Back then, there was a lot."

She raised an eyebrow at him. "You didn't read your fan mail?"

He smiled at her. "No. I was too busy pining over a girl back home."

"Stop." She laughed and leaned over to kiss him. "You have no idea how happy it makes me to know that you missed me. After getting no responses, I was pretty pissed at you."

He tugged her back down into the warmth of the bed and wrapped his arm around her, pulling her against him. "Trust me, I do know how you felt, Zin. Though I wasn't pissed, just heartbroken."

"Liar," she said without any heat and then turned and brushed a kiss over his lips.

"It's all true," he whispered, cupping her breast with one hand and then kissing her shoulder.

"Hmm," she murmured and pressed her hips back against him. "I could get used to this."

His heart swelled with pure pleasure. Everything he'd thought he'd known for the last decade regarding her and their relationship had been wrong. And now that he knew the truth, he had to make up for some lost time. "So could I, gorgeous. What do you say we do this all again tonight? Eight o'clock?"

She placed her hand over his and slowly started to guide him down until he felt her soft curls between his fingers. "What about right now?"

His entire body hardened, and as he dipped his fingers into her, finding her already wet, he whispered, "Jesus, Zinnia. Are you trying to make me lose my mind?"

"No." She let out a soft, contented sigh. "I just don't want to send you off to work without something to remember me by."

He chuckled in her ear. "Trust me. I won't forget. Not ever."

"Let's just make sure, shall we?" She twisted in his arms, pushed him onto his back, and climbed on top of him.

He grinned up at her. "You're going to make me late for my call time."

She wrapped her hand around the base of his cock and positioned it at her opening. "Do you care?"

"God no," he rasped, his voice suddenly hoarse.

"Good." She sank down onto him and watched his eyes roll into the back of his head as his hands tightened on her hips.

FOUR ORGASMS between them and two hours later, Zinnia walked him to the door. Reed was dressed, but she was still in her bathrobe, her hair wet from the shower they'd taken together.

He paused and kissed her one last time. "I'll be here by eight tonight and not a minute later."

She gazed up at him, wondering if she was going to wake up from some sort of magical spell and realize their time together had just been one fantastic dream. The past twenty-four hours seemed unbelievable to her, but as she pressed her hand against his chest and felt his steadily beating heart, she was convinced this was real. How could it not be? She could feel him already occupying a place in her heart. "I'll be waiting."

His eyes glinted with heat. "I'm going to be hearing those words replaying over and over in my mind all day. Just do me a favor, will you?"

"Anything."

"Wear your sexiest underwear so I can rip it off you the moment I see you."

She laughed.

He didn't.

"Oh. You're serious," she said.

"Very. I'm going to be imagining you in black lace all day. And when I get back here tonight, well… just be ready for me."

She placed her hands on her hips. "And who's going to replace this underwear?"

"Don't you worry about that, Zin. I've already decided to restock whatever we ruin and add a little bit to the collection. What do you say?"

Heat travelled all over her body as she imagined him making good on his threat. She cleared her throat. "I say yes."

"Good." He pulled her to him one more time, kissed her until her head began to spin, and then opened the door before he even let go.

Chatter erupted immediately as flashes of light blinded her.

"Reed, what will Krissy say when she learns about your new mystery girl?" someone shouted.

"Do you and Krissy have an open relationship?"

"What does this mean for *Engaged to a Werewolf*? Will you still be able to work together?"

The questions continued in rapid fire, one after another until finally, Reed slammed the door shut and turned to Zinnia. In a very low, controlled tone, he said, "Tell me it wasn't you who called them."

"It wasn't me who called them." There was fury in his eyes, and though she was pretty sure his ire wasn't directed at her, she took a step back just to put some distance between them. "I would never do that to you. Or us."

He closed his eyes and took a deep breath. "Right. I knew that. I just don't know who did."

"Does it matter?" she asked.

"Of course it does," he said, staring at her like she had three heads. "You don't want the tabloids recording your every move, do you?"

"No. But is it the end of the world if they find out you're with me?" she shot back, more than a little offended he seemed so upset that they'd been caught on film.

"Find out... what? No." Realization dawned in his expression, and he moved in, wrapping his arms around her again. "I don't care who knows about us. In fact, I'm rather anxious to show you off. I just hate having every private moment of my life on display for the world. You, my lovely girl, are one I wanted to keep all to myself for a while for my own selfish reasons. Do you understand?"

"I think so," she said with a nod. Their night together had been special and none of anyone else's business. She began to understand what he had to deal with on a daily basis and the price he paid just for being a good actor.

"I have to say something to them," he said, running a hand through his hair.

"Why?" They'd write whatever they wanted to anyway.

"Because if I don't, you're going to be cast as the other woman in this nonexistent triangle with Krissy. I need to set the record straight."

"I don't care what they say about me," Zinnia said with a shrug.

"I know, gorgeous," he said, giving her an affectionate smile. "But I do."

He bent and kissed her on the cheek, and before she could say another word, he flung the door open and walked out onto her porch.

CHAPTER 9

"Holy shit! You're famous." Frankie pushed her long dark curls out of her face as she strode into the back room of Zinnia's shop. Without missing a beat, she hopped up and sat on the stainless steel workstation directly across from where Zinnia was putting the finishing touches on the third round of werewolf cookies. This time Zinnia had skipped the butt portrait and had recreated a headshot of Reed in his wolf form.

"More like notorious," Zinnia said, making a face at her sister.

"At least you look hot." Frankie waved the tabloid in front of Zinnia's face. "Look at you. Your cheeks are flushed, and you have that contented look a woman gets when she's been ridden hard and put away wet."

"Frankie!" Zinnia's cheeks flushed with heat and she wished more than anything she could just hole up in her house for the next two months until Reed's show finished filming and all of the paparazzi left town. The only problem was that Reed would leave with them, and when that day came, she knew she'd be heartbroken all over again. Despite Reed's assurances that he wasn't going to let her go this time, she still feared her calls and letters would go unanswered once they were living three thousand miles away from each other.

It had been only twenty-four hours since the pictures had hit the gossip columns and newsstands. Her life hadn't been her own since. She'd had to turn her phone off and sneak out in the middle of the night through the woods just to avoid the paparazzi who'd been camped out at the end of her driveway ever since Reed had walked out onto her porch and proclaimed that she was his girlfriend. He'd shut down any questions about Krissy, indicating to the press that they weren't together and never had been.

Now there were articles in the same tabloids speculating about Krissy's sexual preference and how she'd likely just been using Reed as a beard. Since Zinnia had seen Krissy and Holly together with her own two eyes, she suspected the rumors were true, but she hadn't said a word to anyone, not even Frankie. Zinnia didn't much care for the actress, but she wasn't interested in getting in the middle of anyone else's business.

"Come on, Zinnia," Frankie said. "Can't you just relax and enjoy this a while? It's not every day a girl gets to sleep with Reed Sinhawk." She fanned herself.

"If I wasn't already married to the love of my life, I'd probably hate you right now."

Zinnia snorted out a laugh. "He mentioned that time you asked him out when you were ten. Remember that?"

Frankie placed a hand over her heart and hunched forward as if she were wounded. "How could I forget? I was devastated for weeks."

The bell indicating someone had stepped into the shop sounded, and Zinnia heard her assistant Greta call out a greeting.

"Where's Zinnia Franklyn?" an angry woman demanded.

"Uh oh." Frankie slid off the counter and moved toward the door. "What did you do this time?"

"Beats me. Maybe it's someone from the set who is angry she's had to wait three days for these cookies," Zinnia said, already removing her apron. "I guess I better go find out."

But before Zinnia could even take one step, the back door flew open and clattered against the wall. Krissy stomped in. Her eyes were puffy and rimmed with smudged mascara. Her sleek hair had turned to a mop of frizz. And to top it off, she was wearing a white shirt with a mustard stain just over her left breast.

"Krissy?" Zinnia asked. "Are you all right?"

"All right?" she mimicked in an impossibly high voice. "'Are you all right,' she asked. Ha! Have you seen the latest gossip rags?"

"We did," Frankie said calmly as she moved to stand

next to her sister. "Everyone knows you can't believe a word they say. Why are you so upset?"

Krissy glared at Zinnia. "It wasn't enough for you that you had to steal my fiancé? You had to go around spreading lies about me, too?"

"Lies? I didn't—" Zinnia started.

"I know what you think you saw back at the set," Krissy said, stalking toward her with her finger out. "But what you don't understand is that we're actors. That's what we do. And we're damned good at it, too. Holly is—well, she was just helping me with a part. Got it?"

"Krissy, I didn't say anything to anyone. Reed's the one—"

"Reed would've never said anything to those vultures. *I know him.* You don't." Krissy glanced down at one of the finished cookies and shook her head in disgust. "You really are just an infatuated fan, aren't you? Pathetic really. Well, you've had your two minutes in the spotlight with Reed. By this time next week, he'll be back in my bed."

"Back in your bed?" Zinnia asked, her stomach churning with the implication. Hadn't Reed told her that he'd never even dated Krissy? *Dating and sleeping together aren't exactly the same thing,* she told herself. She felt the blood drain from her face and had to clutch at the table to keep from losing her balance. She knew Reed hadn't been celibate for the last decade. Considering his impressive skills, she was grateful for that. But she sure as hell didn't want to know about his conquests, especially if they involved Krissy.

Krissy snapped her fingers and a small man wearing a green suit with matching green bowler hat hurried into the room. He stopped right in front of her and bowed as if she were royalty. "At your service, Miss Kimble."

Zinnia and Frankie shared a quizzical glance. Who was this? Her own personal leprechaun?

"Give her the letter." Krissy pointed at Zinnia.

"Yes, ma'am." The leprechaun pulled an unmarked envelope from the inside pocket of his jacket and held it out. "Are you Miss Zinnia Franklyn?"

"Yes. Why?" she said.

"This is for you, courtesy of Mr. Sinhawk."

"Reed sent me a letter?" she asked, gingerly taking the envelope. Instantly her blood ran cold. *He'd sent a letter with Krissy? That couldn't be good.*

"It's from his father," Frankie said, a scowl on her face as she moved to stand protectively in front of Zinnia.

"What?" Zinnia asked, but she already knew. Her sister was a seer and must've just had a vision of what they'd find when they opened the letter.

Krissy craned her neck so that she could see around Frankie and gave Zinnia a cat-that-ate-the canary grin and said, "You've been served."

Zinnia's fist curled around the envelope, crumpling the paper. "For what?"

"Lying about me to the media. No one says shit

about me and gets away with it. My future father-in-law is making sure my reputation isn't damaged further. Reed will see soon enough how you've used him to sell information to the tabloids, and then he'll come running back to me."

"You little bitch—" Zinnia started, but her sister cut her off.

"I think you've made your point," Frankie said, taking a step toward the actress. "Reed can make his own choices. In the meantime, please refrain from insulting my sister, or I'll instruct my ghoul to haunt you day and night."

"You're lying," Krissy said, narrowing her eyes at Frankie.

"Oh really? Haven't you ever heard rumors of Heather Jean Mansfield?" Frankie asked her, referring to their fourth cousin twice removed. She'd died five years ago and had haunted Frankie's bookshop ever since. When Heather Jean didn't like someone, she did her level best to run them off and had acquired quite the notorious reputation. The truth was she was mostly harmless, but Krissy wouldn't know that.

Unease flickered in Krissy's eyes, but when she blinked it was gone, replaced by indifference. "Whatever. Let's go," she said to the leprechaun and then turned on her heel and stalked out. The little man ran after her, and a second later, they heard the bell chime on the front door, indicating they'd left the building.

"She's insane," Zinnia said.

"No doubt, but she's managed to get Reed's father on her side. I think you better open that letter," Frankie said.

Zinnia glanced down at the envelope in her hand and felt as if she was going to vomit. Did Reed know what was going on? He couldn't, could he? Surely he'd have warned her. The fact that she didn't know the answers to those questions made a pit form in her stomach. She glanced up at Frankie. "How did I get myself into this mess?"

Frankie gave her sister a gentle smile. "I believe it was when you threw caution to the wind and allowed that hot man to give you mind-blowing orgasms."

"Right." And the fact was Zinnia didn't regret her choice at all. She couldn't. She loved Reed, and nothing short of him being in cahoots with Krissy would change that. She dug her phone out of her pocket and hit Reed's number. It went straight to voicemail. *Dammit*, she thought and typed out a text.

I just had a visit from Krissy. Need to talk to you. Call me back ASAP. She hit Send and sighed when there was no immediate reply.

Frankie grabbed the envelope from her sister and tore it open. "Do you want to read it or should I?"

"You do it," Zinnia said, bracing herself.

Frankie scanned the letter and swore.

"Oh gods. It's really bad, isn't it?" Zinnia said.

"Yes. There's a letter from Reed's father and his attorney. Reed's father is paying his attorney to represent Krissy in a defamation suit. It says here he won't stand for his future daughter-in-law to be humiliated by a gold-digging fan."

"What the hell? I didn't say anything to anyone about Krissy, and I've never taken a dime from anyone. The studio hasn't even paid me for these cookies yet!" Zinnia cried.

Frankie reached out and squeezed her sister's hand. "I'm so sorry, Zin. There's a copy of a sworn statement from Krissy that says you threatened to go to the gossip rags and tell them she's dating a woman if she didn't stay away from Reed. She's suing you for defamation of character for five million dollars."

Zinnia's world spun. *"Five million dollars?"*

Frankie just nodded.

"I could work for another hundred years and never even get close to that. Who are they kidding?" Zinnia paced around her work table, her fingers worrying her apron. "And that sworn statement is total bullshit. I never said a word about Holly to anyone. Not Krissy, not Reed, not the press. They must've found out from someone else who works on the set, because it sure as hell wasn't me."

"That's true?" Frankie exclaimed. "Holy shit. Krissy has a *girlfriend?*"

"Uh… maybe? I saw her making out with a woman named Holly. I also managed to overhear them fighting about their relationship. So they might be girlfriends, but they might've also broken up. That's hardly the point anyway. Who cares if Krissy is into women? The point is that I never said anything to anyone until this very moment."

"The point is, dear sister, that if it's true that Krissy was dating a woman, even if you did talk to someone, it can't be defamation. Which means this lawsuit is an even bigger pile of shit than I originally thought." Frankie strode over to where the last of the werewolf cookies were still sitting on their trays and started stuffing them into the box.

Zinnia, not knowing what else to do with herself, joined in, and the two of them worked in silence until the box was full.

Frankie stacked the three boxes, but before Zinnia could grab them, Frankie put her hand out. "Nope. I'm taking these to the set. Don't you worry about a thing, big sister. I'm going to handle not just the cookies, but your Krissy problem, too."

Zinnia narrowed her eyes. "What are you planning?"

"Just a little something that will take down that entitled little crotch scratcher a notch or five."

Zinnia snorted and couldn't help the laugh that followed. "You need to keep that to yourself. Reed told me that in confidence, and if that gets out, I really will be in trouble."

"Yeah, I know. But when it's just us, that's gonna be her nickname forevermore." Frankie grinned at her sister, tightened her grip on the cookies, and strode out.

CHAPTER 10

Zinnia jammed the paperwork in her purse and headed home. By the time she passed the caravan of photographers at the end of her driveway, she was so pissed she was seeing red. How had they even known Reed was with her the other night?

The same way the photographer found us at the hot springs, Zinnia thought. Krissy had told them. There was no reason to believe Krissy hadn't known where Reed was going after the shoot. He hadn't made a secret of the two of them seeing each other. The question was, why? What was in it for Krissy to make her and Reed's affair public?

Zinnia had no answers other than the actress was a terrible person. Once she was inside the house, Zinnia headed straight for her wine cellar. If ever there was a time for a drink, it was now. She sat down at the bar in her kitchen and proceeded to drink the afternoon away. Once she was two-thirds of the way through the bottle, her sister called to check in on her.

"Are you okay?" Frankie asked.

"Better now that I've made friends with a ten-year-old bottle of cabernet."

"Oh no. You and wine aren't the best combination when you're in this state. Just try to keep out of the kitchen, okay? We don't need you concocting another one of your revenge potions."

"Hey, now you're talking," Zinnia said, wondering why she hadn't thought of that already. Zinnia had excelled at creating potions in school. It was one of her talents.

"No. Don't even think about it," Frankie said. "Remember the last time you made one while drunk? You gave old man Parker a rash on his genitals because he told you your cupcakes were too lumpy."

"He deserved it though, Frankie," she slurred. "He was talking about my tits!"

"True, but I don't think crafting a potion to curse the person suing you is a good idea. Promise me you won't do that," her sister ordered.

"Okay, fine. I won't. Now why did you call? Did you need some cookies?" Zinnia asked, her head spinning from the wine.

"No. Never mind. I'll see you in a few hours."

"Okay, hurry. Otherwise all of the wine will be gone." Zinnia hiccupped into the phone and giggled. "Oops."

"Oh boy. You're a mess. Put the wine down and try to eat something. Okay?"

"Sure, sis. See you soon." Zinnia ended the call, glanced at her empty wine glass and filled it again. Her body was warm and tingly all over, and she could barely remember why she was so upset. What was it again?

Krissy's smirking face flashed in her mind. "Right," Zinnia said to no one. "That buttface is trying to sue me." She slid off her chair and stumbled over to her pantry. "I can't let her get away with that."

Her sister's voice echoed in her mind... something about potions and giving old man Parker a genital rash. She giggled. "That's exactly what Krissy deserves. Another genital rash."

Unfortunately, she couldn't recall the rash potion. But she did have something else in mind. Still giggling to herself, Zinnia started rummaging around in her cabinets, intent on making Krissy the perfect potion.

REED GLANCED at the text from Zinnia and nearly came apart as rage filled him. It'd come in over an hour ago when he'd been in a meeting with the studio heads about the tabloid scandal. They were pissed because they'd been promoting him and Krissy as a happily engaged couple for the upcoming season, and all their marketing had just gone to shit. But he didn't give two flying fucks what they thought. It wasn't in his contract that he had to be dating or in a real relationship with his co-star. And frankly, he was damned tired of everyone telling him what to do when it came to his love life.

As soon as he'd walked out of the meeting, he'd taken a call from his manager who'd warned him about the lawsuit and the fact that his father was behind it. It was after that call when he first saw her text. He wanted to call her, knew she deserved as much, but he was far too angry in that moment. Instead he texted back. *I just heard. Don't worry. I'll handle it.*

There was no immediate reply. He waited a few more minutes then added a second text. *Fuck the paparazzi. I'll be there as soon as I can.*

They'd decided to lay low for a bit until the photographers gave up on stalking her house, but after the day he'd had, he was completely over it. The press wasn't going to keep him away from his girl for a moment longer than necessary. Neither was his controlling bastard of a father. He shoved the phone into his pocket and strode into the large Victorian's parlor where Remington Sinhawk was holding a glass of scotch while reassuring Krissy's father that the latest scandal would be dead and buried within hours.

"Reed, there you are." Philip Kimble clapped him on the back. "It's an unfortunate mess you seem to have gotten yourself into with that bakery woman. I can't say I blame you though. She sure has a great ass on her, doesn't she? I bet she's a wildcat and crazy in the sack." He leaned in and leered like only a sick fuck could.

"The quiet ones always are. Next time be sure to choose someone a little more discrete. But don't worry. Remington and I know how to handle the ones who talk too much."

"What the fuck did you just say?" Reed shrugged the other man off and curled his own hand into a fist, ready to break the other man's face.

Philip's expression darkened, and a vein popped out on his neck as all his muscles tensed. "Don't tell me you're more into that little whore than you are my daughter. Because I'll rip your head off if you embarrass her one more time."

"Call Zinnia a whore one more time and we'll see whose head gets ripped off," Reed said with a growl.

"That's enough," Remington Sinhawk said, stepping between the two men. He turned to Philip. "If you want my help, you'll stop provoking my son."

The other man continued to glare at Reed, but when he finally glanced at Remington, he backed off.

"Reed," Remington said, disappointment dripping in his tone. "What *are* you doing with that girl? Do you have any idea what this looks like to the public? They will turn on Krissy if she stays with a serial cheater. You know that won't play well during the campaign."

"I don't give a fuck about the goddamned campaign," Reed roared. "And for the last time, I'm not *with* Krissy. I never was. She knows that. You know that. And so does her opportunistic father over there. What do I have to do to get the three of you to stop pushing this insane narrative that we're going to marry for the good of the families. This isn't the Victorian era for Christ's sake."

Remington Sinhawk's expression turned from mildly irritated to full-on angry in two seconds flat. He kept his gaze locked on his son's, and in a low, barely control tone, he asked, "Are you telling me you don't care about the next election?"

Reed knew that look. He'd been on the receiving end of his father's wrath more than a handful of times after defying his father's wishes. But he was done. Over it. His father was a US Senator who never spoke to Reed unless he needed him to charm a donor or soften his public image. Not anymore. He was done and willing to risk the fallout, if not for himself, then certainly for Zinnia. "If it means pretending to love someone I can barely stand talking to, then yes, that's exactly what I'm saying, Father."

A small gasp came from behind him followed by the barest whisper. "Reed, I can't believe you just said that."

He rolled his eyes and turned around to glare at his costar. "Yes, you can, Krissy. How dare you sue Zinnia and accuse her of outing you. The entire production crew has been gossiping all day about how they all knew about you and Holly. And don't think they won't testify on Zinnia's behalf if you drag her to court. Half of them can't stand you. And the other half, the local half, are very protective of her. This isn't going to go well for you, especially if you want those rumors to blow over."

"Wha…what?" she stammered as she glanced at her father.

He had been glaring at Reed since their altercation, but now he was looking at his daughter with a furrowed brow and a confused expression on his face.

"It's not true, Daddy." She rushed over to him. "He's just trying to turn everyone against me because he's mad that I'm suing that girl he's been in love with forever."

"He's not lying," another woman said from the doorway. Holly leaned against the doorframe, a pained expression on her face. "Krissy is terrified to go public with our relationship, but I can't stand by and let her ruin another woman's life because she is too scared of what the public thinks. Mr. Kimble, your daughter and I have been a couple for over two years. But that's all about to change. I won't do this to myself anymore." She turned her gaze on her girlfriend. "I'm done. You've crossed a line I'm not willing to accept."

"Holly! I—" Krissy started, but then she glanced at her father and promptly closed her mouth.

"Is this true, Kris?" her father asked, his expression blank.

She opened her mouth, closed it, and then just stared at her feet.

Holly let out a long sigh. "Goodbye, Kat" She spun around, her sleek black hair flying out behind her as she took off down the hall.

"Holly, wait!" Krissy ran after her, grabbed the other woman's hand, and hauled her back into the room. "I'm so sorry, my love. Don't go. I'll just die if you go. You have to give me another chance."

Holly glanced at Krissy's father. "Are you telling me you're finally going to be honest with him?"

Tears rolled down Krissy's cheeks as she nodded. "I think the cat is definitely out of the bag."

Reed watched in silence as Mr. Kimble moved toward his daughter. But instead of being angry or lashing out at his daughter's revelation, he held his hand out to her and pulled her into his arms.

She sobbed and buried her head into his chest. "I'm so sorry, Daddy. I just didn't want to disappoint you."

"Shh," the man said quietly. "You could never disappoint me, Buttercup. There's no need to cry. It's okay. Everything is going to be just fine." He glanced over his daughter's head and eyed Holly. "Do you love my daughter?"

"Yes, sir," Holly said as she inched closer to Reed.

He could sense the fear coming off her and tried to smile reassuringly at her. But who could blame her? He knew all too well how both his father and Krissy's could make someone's life hell when they didn't approve of something.

"Tell me something about yourself and your family," Mr. Kimble said, patting his daughter's back in a reassuring gesture.

Holly glanced at Reed, panic in her expressive eyes. They both knew what Philip was after. He wanted to know if Holly had family connections he could exploit. Reed shrugged one shoulder and said, "You might as well tell him. He'll likely do a background check anyway."

Philip visibly stiffened and started eyeing her with suspicion. "Do you have a troubled past, young lady?"

"No, Daddy," Krissy said, tilting her head up to look at him. "Holly lost both of her parents when she was eighteen and only has a great aunt who lives out in Montana. She's a retired nurse. Holly put herself through design school and everything she has, she's worked for herself. It's really admirable."

The actress's face had lit up while she was talking about Holly, and the love there was unmistakable to Reed. It was a side he hadn't seen of her except when they'd been in front of the camera. "She loves you," he whispered to Holly.

The costume designer nodded. "That was never the issue."

"Design school?" Mr. Kimble asked. "Impressive." He walked over to Holly and reached out to shake her hand. "I've always admired hard workers. Tell me, young lady, have you ever thought of designing your own clothing line?"

"Thank you." Holly shook his hand and then started talking about how she'd always wanted to work on a collection but didn't have time in her schedule.

Mr. Kimble nodded and then wrapped his free arm around Holly's shoulders. With both girls in his arms, he started making plans for how to help Holly with her career goals.

Krissy and Holly beamed at each other, both clearly

just as surprised as Reed about how easily Mr. Kimble had accepted his daughter's news.

"Daddy?" Krissy asked.

"Yes, Buttercup?"

"Does this mean you accept my relationship with Holly?"

He seemed startled by her question. "Of course, Krissy. Why wouldn't I?"

"Because…" She swallowed. "Mama is going to freak."

His light eyes darkened, and it was clear that Mrs. Kimble wasn't nearly as open-minded as Philip. "You just let me handle your mother. No one is going to make my girl feel like she's doing something wrong. Not even your mother."

Another tear rolled down Krissy's cheek.

Philip wiped it away. "Shh now. All I've ever wanted was for you to be happy, and if Holly makes you happy, then I'm on board. There's only one thing we have to take care of first, though."

Krissy stiffened. "What's that?"

"We need to go over to Ms. Franklyn's house. You're going to let her know you're dropping the lawsuit, and then you're going to apologize."

"Apologize!" Krissy said, returning to her normally selfish demeanor.

Reed rolled his eyes. "That's not necessary. I can relay a message."

"No, I think Mr. Kimble is right," Holly said. "Zinnia deserves to hear this from Krissy."

"She's right, Buttercup," Philip said, unyielding to his daughter's selfishness. "You'll apologize, or you're on your own."

While Reed was glad to see Philip setting boundaries for his daughter, he couldn't get over the blatant hypocrisy. Less than ten minutes ago, he'd been talking shit about Zinnia and was ready to go along with Remington's plan as long as it benefited his daughter. And now he was enforcing some sort of moral high road? It was enough to make one's head spin. Even so, he needed Krissy to drop the lawsuit, and he was going to make sure it happened, with zero chance of resurfacing.

"She should be home. We can go now," Reed said and turned to his father. "All of us. Dad get your lawyer on the phone. I want this to be finished today."

"I don't think you need me. This is your mess, Reed," his father said.

Reed growled, actually *growled*, at his father.

The other man blinked. "Are you challenging me?"

"No, but I will. I wouldn't be in this *mess* if it wasn't for you butting in where you didn't belong," Reed said. "Call the lawyer. Have him meet us at Zinnia's place, or the shit is really going to hit the fan when I start granting interviews to all the gossip rags. And when they ask about you, I won't hesitate to mention that affair you had just after Reese died."

His father's face turned an unpleasant shade of red. "If you do that, it'll kill your mother."

Reed let out a huff of humorless laughter. If anyone

had been able to break his mother, it would've been Remington Sinhawk, the man who basically ignored her for the last fifteen years while he pretended Reese had never existed. He always changed the subject when Brooke Sinhawk talked about her oldest son and shut down any reporters who asked about him. "Nice try, Dad. But she's stronger than you give her credit for."

"I wouldn't bet on that." But he pulled out his phone, sent a text, and then added, "The lawyer is on his way. Let's get this over with so I can get back to work. This little side trip has cost me more than time."

Even though Reed's blood was boiling and he was itching for a fight with his father, he kept his temper in check. Zinnia was more important.

CHAPTER 11

"*Z*in?" Reed's voice seemed far away, but Zinnia could smell his faint woodsy scent and smiled. "Wake up, love. I have good news."

This time his voice was clearer, and she opened her eyes, blinking to clear her blurry vision. "Reed?" Her voice was raspy, and she sounded like she'd been on an all-night bender. Though, she had downed at least an entire bottle of wine all on her own, so technically she had been on a bender.

"There you are." He smiled down at her and brushed a lock of hair out of her eyes. "Looks like you started the party without me," he said gently.

She sat up and pressed a hand to her queasy stomach. "Oh, no. That's not good."

Alarm flashed across his features. "Are you going to be sick?"

She clutched the armrest of her couch and shook

her head. "No. But I could use a bottle of my fortifying potion. It's in the fridge, behind the milk."

"I'll be right back." He rose from the couch and strode into the next room. It was then she noticed Krissy was there. The moment their eyes met, Krissy scurried after him and disappeared into the kitchen.

"Bitch," Zinnia muttered. Someone cleared their throat, and Zinnia nearly jumped right out of her skin. With her heart racing, she scanned the room, finding Holly, Reed's father, and two other men she didn't know all congregated near her front door.

"That's my daughter you're talking about," a round, bald man said in a disapproving tone.

"You can't really blame her for being upset," Holly said to him. "Krissy did try to sue her for five million dollars."

The man bristled and pursed his lips. "Even so, she's still my daughter."

Holly patted him on the arm and moved across the room to sit next to Zinnia on the couch. "Are you all right?"

"I will be as soon as I get my potion and find out why everyone has invaded my house."

"Krissy is here to apologize," she said. "Me, too. I had no idea she would do something like that. It wasn't right."

The tall, polished man standing next to Reed's father came forward, holding a yellow folder out to Zinnia. "Inside, you'll find the paperwork indicating the suit will be dropped. There is also a settlement agreement stating the matter has been resolved and that neither party will refile regarding comments involving Ms. Kimble's personal life to this date. And there's the standard nondisclosure clause, of course."

"Of course." Zinnia took the paperwork, but her head was still too fuzzy for her to process what was happening. Had they just offered to settle? Were they expecting her to pay some sort of damages? She was about to ask when Reed reappeared with her potion.

"Here. I also got you some toast, just in case," he said.

"Thanks." She smiled weakly at him, downed a couple of gulps of the potion, and then nibbled on the toast.

He sat down next to her. "It's over. She's dropping the suit."

Zinnia nodded to the folder. "Have you read that?"

"Yes."

"How much do they want?" She took another sip of the potion, and her head started to clear.

"What do you mean?" He snatched the folder and glared at his father. "Did someone tell her she has to pay Krissy even though her suit is total bullshit?"

The lawyer shook his head. "No. There's no payment stipulation."

"Of course there isn't," Krissy said as she bounced back into the room. "Even I wouldn't try something that crazy." She put a hand over her mouth as she giggled. "Okay, I probably would, but I'm trying to change. Holly doesn't like it when I'm a bitch."

Holly rolled her eyes. "Krissy, what are you doing?"

Krissy flopped down on the other side of Zinnia. "I'm so sorry for this lawsuit business. You didn't deserve that. I was just... well, you know. Scared. My career. My parents. I've never really felt like I can just be myself."

Zinnia frowned at the woman. Her eyes were too wide, and she was talking too fast, almost as if she were on some sort of drug. "Are you high?"

"What?" She blinked, and Zinnia noticed her pupils were slightly dilated. "No. I don't do drugs. Unless you count caffeine. I'm definitely addicted to coffee. And that mocha concoction you had in your fridge, wow, did it taste awesome. If there'd been enough, I'd have probably bathed in it, it was so good."

"Mocha...?" Zinnia frowned. "I didn't—oh no. You didn't drink the stuff that was in the pitcher, did you?"

"Yeah, why? Were you saving it for someone else? I'll get you more if you like. I didn't mean to—"

"It's a truth potion," Zinnia said, cutting her off. The one she'd made intending to spike Krissy's drink in order to trap the woman into confessing the lawsuit was a sham. She must've perfected the part that lured Krissy to the drink. She hadn't been in her house more than a couple of minutes before she'd been drawn to it like a moth to a flame. *Damn, I'm good*, Zinnia thought. *Maybe I should get drunk and brew more often.*

"That explains why I feel so free," Krissy said and

laid her head on Zinnia's shoulder. "I'm so sorry for causing all this trouble. I never meant to sue you, you know. I hired that photographer to follow you to the hot springs so that when the pictures surfaced, I could get out of that awful engagement to Reed. He's good looking and all, but we just don't do it for each other."

Zinnia nodded. She'd suspected as much about the photographer, but that didn't explain the lawsuit. "So why did you try to sue me?"

She let out a heavy sigh. "My dad lost his mind when the tabloids hit. He called Mr. Sinhawk, and then everything just got away from me. I shouldn't have gone along with it. I really am sorry."

"Jesus," Reed muttered, shaking his head at the men still standing by the door. "Don't you two have any shame?"

"I was just protecting my daughter," Philip said with a shrug.

"It's the way the world works, Reed. You know that," Remington said. "Don't be so naïve."

Zinnia and Reed shared a mutual look of disgust, but before either could say anything, Krissy started to stroke Zinnia's leg. Zinnia tried to pull away, but Krissy just inched closer.

"You're really sexy, you know that?" the actress said. "I can see why Reed is so infatuated with you."

"Okay. That's enough," Holly said, holding out a hand to her girlfriend. "Time to go."

Krissy looked up at her and beamed. "Do you know how I first knew I was a lesbian?"

Holly shook her head. "That's probably a conversation for another time."

"It was when Vinny Vanderhoff and I were making out and he asked me to suck his penis. I was so thoroughly creeped out that I vomited on him the moment he whipped it out. Have you seen those things? My god, they are really creepy. It's like they're just looking at you, begging for attention like a needy little worm."

Reed choked out a laugh and it was all Zinnia could do to not join him. Good goddess, that potion had turned out to be entertaining. And she hadn't even stooped to giving her enemy a nasty rash. She felt as if she was growing.

"Krissy. That's not appropriate conversation," her dad admonished.

"Oh, please, Dad. Don't think I don't remember that time I walked in on you and mom during your swinger phase. You know all about weird penises, don't you? I seem to recall you messing with the football player and mom getting down with the cheerleader." She leaned into Holly and stage-whispered, "I guess the homo tendencies run deep in this family."

"I never—" Philip started but then stopped, his face going so red Zinnia thought he might explode right there in her living room.

"Get over it, Dad," Krissy said. "No one cares anyway." She took the file out of Reed's hands, flipped it open and signed both documents. Then she looked at the lawyer. "Do you need anything else?"

"Nope. I think that just about covers it." He nodded to Zinnia. "Once you sign, we'll be done here."

"I need to read it over," Zinnia said, more than a little uncomfortable. She'd been caught off guard, and not only did she want to read it, she wanted her own lawyer to take a look.

"No problem." Krissy patted her leg. "Take your time. I'm going to go so Holly and I can have makeup sex." She smiled suggestively at Holly, stood, and held her hand out to her girlfriend. "Ready?"

Holly laughed as she took Krissy's hand and got to her feet. "You have no idea."

"Dad, let's go," Krissy said. Once the three of them were at the door, she paused and waved at Reed. "I know you're pissed at me. I know I deserve it. But do you think you might ever forgive me? I'd really like us to be friends again someday."

Reed glanced at Zinnia, raising one eyebrow in question.

She nodded. "I think it's best if we just all put this behind us. I think it's safe to say that coming out has been a little traumatic for her. I'm willing to forgive and forget if you are. Besides, you two still need to work together."

Reed took her hand in his and squeezed her fingers. Then he turned his attention to Krissy. "I'll forgive, but I won't forget. If anything like this happens again, I'll leave the show for good. Understood?"

Her face broke out into a relieved smile. "Thanks,

Reed. It won't. I'm a changed woman." Krissy glanced up at Holly. "Or at least I'm working on it."

Holly bent and kissed her softly on the lips while Philip continued to silently fume. Then the three of them disappeared out the front door, leaving Reed and Zinnia alone with Remington and his lawyer.

CHAPTER 12

"Well, young lady, if you'll just sign those papers then we can get back on the road," Remington Sinhawk said as he tapped his fingers on the entry table. His obvious irritation made Reed's skin crawl. How many times had he watched his father behave exactly like that when he'd been a child? He behaved as if his time was precious and everyone else was inconveniencing him. The message was clear. Remington was important—more important than anyone else.

"I'd rather have my lawyer look over everything first," Zinnia said as she scanned the papers.

Remington gritted his teeth. "Leonard and I don't have all day to spend on this foolishness."

Reed came off the couch as if he had a rocket attached to his ass. "She has every right to get her legal contracts vetted by her own lawyer, Father."

Before Remington could respond, the door opened,

and Frankie strode in with Reed's mother in tow. Brooke Sinhawk was dressed in a cream linen suit. Her hair was tied back into a sleek blond ponytail, and her makeup was flawless, as always. On the runway, she'd been known as the ice queen. But as his mother, she'd never been anything but warm and nurturing. Reed often wondered what she saw in his father. It was a question he knew would never be answered.

"Reed!" She threw her arms around him and hugged him tightly. "I came as soon as I heard what was going on. Are you all right? What about Zinnia?"

"She's doing better now," Reed said as she released him. "What are you doing here?"

"Making sure you and your father don't kill each other," she said in a matter-of-fact tone. Then she spotted Zinnia and headed straight for her with her arms out. *She always did like Zinnia,* Reed thought. And it pleased him to watch the two women he loved more than anyone else in the world embrace each other.

"It's been way too long, Zinnia dear," his mother said with a sniff.

"I've missed you too," Zin said, her eyes misting with emotion. "How did you know where to find us?"

Brooke released her from the embrace and dabbed at her eyes. "I ran into Frankie at the set. She said she'd heard everyone was here, so we jumped in the car and well... here we are."

"Someone needs to fill us in," Frankie said. "We ran into Krissy, Holly, and Krissy's father, but other than hearing all about Krissy's plans in the bedroom later, we didn't get much in the way of details." She stared pointedly at her sister. "I told you not to make any potions. Do you want to explain how Krissy ended up downing a truth serum?"

Zinnia raised her hands in a surrender motion. "It's totally not my fault. She found it and drank it without any help from me."

"Right." Frankie sounded skeptical, but she turned her attention to Reed. "Details please. What exactly is this little meeting about?"

He quickly filled them both in and didn't hesitate to throw his father under the bus. "Remington is pissed because Zinnia's desire to have her lawyer go over the documents is inconveniencing him. But never mind the fact that all of this is happening because he butted in where he didn't belong in the first place."

"I was trying to save you from making a huge mistake with someone beneath your station," Remington roared, his voice booming through Zinnia's house. "When will you learn you aren't like everyone else. You can't just do anything or *anyone* you want to!"

Silence hung in the air as everyone turned to stare at Senator Sinhawk.

Reed felt himself start to tremble with the need to shift. The rage was so strong, the urge to protect the one he loved so intense, he could barely think straight. He knew that if his wolf took over, that was it. He'd attack his father and wouldn't stop until one of them was dead. No wolf insulted another's mate without consequences. Reed's blood hummed, and a growl came from deep in his throat. He was right on the edge, but then his mother put her cool hand on his arm, steadying him, calming him just enough that he was able to keep his wolf in line.

"Remington Sinhawk," Brooke said, her tone deadly serious. "What is wrong with you? Have you always been such a shameless elitist? Or is this new now that you think you're going to run for president some day?"

"Now, Brooke. Come on. You know I don't think there is anything wrong with being middle class," he said, trying and failing to soothe his wife's feathers.

She scoffed. "Clearly you do if you need to clarify your position to your wife and son." Brooke turned to Zinnia. "I'm so sorry, darling. Remington has clearly lost all sense of decency. Please do not judge my son based on his father's shortcomings."

Zinnia gave his mother a tentative smile. "I don't. Reed is... well, he's always been wonderful."

Reed felt his heart nearly explode with love for her. His wolf yearned for her, and he couldn't imagine one more day without her. He knew it probably wasn't the best moment, but he just couldn't wait any longer to make her his. With his gaze locked on the woman he loved, he pulled his brother's class ring, the one thing he had left of Reese, off his ring finger and kneeled in front of Zinnia.

She let out a small gasp when he took her left hand and positioned the ring at the tip of her finger. "Reed—"

"Shh. I have a few things to say." He stroked her

finger as he smiled nervously at her. "I've known since I was sixteen who I was meant to spend the rest of my life with. I just didn't know how to deal with that as a young man who was suddenly thrust into stardom. But the moment I heard you were here on this island, nothing could keep me away from you. Not my father, not Krissy, not the press. You're my one, Zinnia. You always have been."

"You're my one, too," Zinnia said, tears rolling unabashedly down her face.

"And I know this is fast. We've only been back in each other's lives for a few days, but we had three years before. I know you, Zin, and I know you know me. The truth is, even if you say no, I'm not going anywhere. I'll be right here by your side for the rest of our lives because you're the only one I feel whole around. The only one I've ever felt whole around. So I'm asking... will you marry me?" He held his breath then gently wiped away her tears as she just gazed at him.

"I know it's asking a lot," he said when she didn't answer. "There's the press and my father's insane political bullshit. But I promise, love, it's going to be me and you forever, always by each other's side. I love you, Zin. The only question is, do you want me?"

"Yes!" she shouted and shoved her finger into the ring he was still holding.

He laughed and then swept her up into a tight hug and twirled her around while kissing her so thoroughly that they were both winded when he finally put her back on her feet.

"Oh, how wonderful!" Brooke said, dabbing at her own tears. "I'm so pleased for you both."

"Brooke, don't encourage this," Remington started.

His wife turned to him, and in one swift motion, she shot a flash of light in his direction. It crackled over his skin then shot down his throat. He opened his mouth to speak, but nothing came out.

Brooke gave him a self-satisfied smile.

"Whoa," Frankie said. "Brooke's a badass."

Brooke winked at her then turned to Reed and Zinnia. Reed stared at his mother in utter shock. "Mom, what did you do?"

"Silencing spell. I'll lift it when he's done being a jackass," she said.

Remington pounded his fist on a side table and looked like he was ready to throttle her.

"I was not going to let you ruin this moment for the only son we have left," she said to him. "We already lost Reese, and if you continue to act like a complete jackass, you're not only going to lose Reed, but me too. I won't stand for it. Do you understand, Remington?"

His eyes narrowed as the two stared each other down. Then finally, Remington gave her the slightest of nods and turned and walked out the door.

"Well," Brooke clapped her hands together. "That could've gone worse."

Reed, overcome with emotion for what his mother had just sacrificed for them both, swept her up in his arms and said, "I love you, Mom."

"I love you, too, son. Now don't waste any time

marrying that gorgeous girl over there. Your wolf won't settle until you do."

"Trust me. I won't." He let go of his mother.

She grabbed Zinnia's hands. "I'm so glad you're going to be part of the family. Don't let Remington get to you. He's certainly shown his ass today, but he wasn't always like this. I have hope he'll come around and figure out it's okay to love again." There was sadness in her tone, but she shook it off and added, "Take as much time as you need to vet those documents and don't let anyone pressure you. If there is one thing I learned being married to a wolf, it's that you need to know how to stand up for yourself. I'm pleased to see you've already mastered that. Don't let it go. It will serve you well."

Brooke kissed both of them on the cheek and then walked out of the house, with Leonard right behind her.

When they were gone, Frankie turned to Reed and Zinnia. "I have the best idea."

Reed wrapped his fingers around Zinnia's and wondered how long it would be until he could get her alone and back into his arms. "What's that, Frankie? Are you headed home to give us some privacy?"

"Yeah, yeah." She rolled her eyes. "But first, what do you think of a Halloween wedding?"

Reed and Zinnia both grinned. That was only a few weeks away. They both nodded, and Reed said, "It's perfect."

CHAPTER 13

"I never imagined you'd get married wearing a black corset dress," Frankie said as she adjusted her sister's boobs to show more cleavage.

Butterflies fluttered in Zinnia's stomach as she swatted her sister's hands away. "I never imagined I'd be marrying my high school crush."

"Oh, please." Frankie rolled her eyes. "That's a blatant lie. You probably daydreamed about this day all the way through senior year."

"No, that was sophomore year," Zinnia said with a wicked grin. "By senior year I was imagining him naked and his tongue—"

"That's quite enough," Krissy said, handing her the blood-red rose bouquet. "No one wants to hear about your Reed fantasies."

"I do," Frankie said, fanning herself.

"Gross. That's your sister's soon to be husband."

Krissy stood back and studied Zinnia's outfit. "You just need one more thing."

Zinnia glanced down at herself. "I'm not going to be able to fit anything else into this dress."

"Not to worry. There's room for this." Krissy, who'd done a one-eighty in the personality department and had been a huge help in getting the wedding together on such short notice, produced a stunning black witch hat complete with diamond-shaped spiders crawling up the side.

"Wow, it's gorgeous," Zinnia said, setting it on top of her red curls. "Where did you get it?"

She shrugged. "I had it sent in from a designer in Paris. It's no big deal."

It very much was a big deal to Zinnia. She knew that Krissy must've had to pull some serious strings to get the must-have fashion accessory of the season sent to a witch none of the designers even knew. Though she supposed her instant fame in the tabloids over the last few weeks hadn't hurt as far as increasing her visibility went. Still, it was a sweet gesture, and Zinnia pulled the other woman in for a hug. "Thank you."

"You're welcome." Krissy stepped back and smoothed her Glinda the Good Witch costume. "I'm just trying to live up to my new image."

"You're doing a damn fine job," Zinnia said.

Frankie shoved a live Venus flytrap bouquet into Krissy's hands and said, "Time to go. We'll meet you out there."

"All right. Good luck," she said to Zinnia and slipped out the door.

Zinnia beamed at her sister. "You look gorgeous, too, you know. Nice touch with the creepy veins and black contacts."

"I always did love Evil Willow," she said, referring to the character from Buffy the Vampire Slayer. "After you two tie the knot, Aron and I are having a Buffy marathon, starting with season six when Buffy and Spike get it on. We probably won't make it that far. That shit is hot."

"Oookay," Zinnia said. "I think I've got the picture."

"Yeah, ya do." Frankie laughed. She grabbed her own Venus flytrap bouquet and walked her sister to the door. "Are you ready for this?"

Zinnia pressed a hand to her abdomen and nodded. "I've been waiting a long time for this day."

"See, I told you. You definitely did imagine marrying him."

"Of course," Zinnia agreed. "I just didn't believe it would happen."

"Well, believe it, because they're playing your song." Frankie kissed her on the cheek and then glided down the aisle to the Adam's Family theme song.

Once Frankie took her place at the edge of the bluff with Krissy and Reed with Aron as his best man, the song changed to Chopin's Death March. She chuckled to herself, and with her head held high, she made her way down the aisle, her heart swelling with so much love she thought it might burst.

Reed's eyes were misted over when she finally made it to his side, but with one glance at her considerable cleavage, they cleared, and he leered at her.

"Are you ready for this, Mr. Sinhawk?" she asked.

He leaned in and whispered, "I've been ready since the first time I saw that impressive rack of yours."

She tilted her head to the side. "And when was that?"

"When you were sixteen and I saw you changing through the window."

"You're a perv."

"Only for you, love." He winked at her then turned his attention to Judge Hawthorne, the same judge who'd married Zinnia's sister Frankie and her husband Aron.

Zinnia couldn't keep her eyes off Reed. He was just so handsome in the moonlight, even in his fake werewolf Halloween costume. His light eyes appeared almost silver, and his perpetual five-o'clock shadow was driving her crazy. She couldn't wait for the ceremony to be over so she could drag him back into her dressing room and have her way with him.

Judging by the way he kept staring at her breasts, he was having the same thoughts.

But then the judge asked them to say their vows, and suddenly having her way with him wasn't nearly as important as professing her undying love and loyalty. By the time they were done, both of them were smiling gently with tears staining their cheeks.

Then suddenly the judge pronounced them

husband and wife and said, "You may now bite the bride."

Zinnia laughed, having forgotten they'd added that part to the ceremony. She'd thought it was a fun touch for a Halloween-themed event. But Reed was looking at her with such intensity, her humor fled and was replaced by something she didn't quite understand.

Longing, loyalty, and pure need hit her all at once and propelled her toward him, right into his arms. Reed breathed her in and ran a light finger down her neck, his touch making her shiver with desire. She wanted to order him to bite her, but she couldn't quite make the words come. Instead, she tilted her head to the side, silently inviting him to take what was his.

Reed ran his tongue over her pulse, then ever so gently bit down on her neck.

Zinnia let out a small gasp as magic skittered over her skin and settled into her bones. Love warmed her from head to toe as she stared into her husband's eyes and smiled.

"Damn," she heard her sister say under her breath. "Now *that's* hot."

"She's right you know," he whispered and then bent his head again and kissed his bride.

Pyper Rayne Novels:
Spirits, Stilettos, and a Silver Bustier
Spirits, Rock Stars, and a Midnight Chocolate Bar
Spirits, Beignets, and a Bayou Biker Gang
Spirits, Diamonds, and a Drive-thru Daiquiri Stand

Jade Calhoun Novels:
Haunted on Bourbon Street
Witches of Bourbon Street
Demons of Bourbon Street
Angels of Bourbon Street
Shadows of Bourbon Street
Incubus of Bourbon Street
Bewitched on Bourbon Street
Hexed on Bourbon Street
Dragons of Bourbon Street

Last Witch Standing Novels:

Soulless at Sunset
Bloodlust By Midnight
Bitten At Daybreak

Crescent City Fae Novels:
Influential Magic
Irresistible Magic
Intoxicating Magic

Witches of Keating Hollow Novels:
Soul of the Witch
Heart of the Witch
Spirit of the Witch
Dreams of the Witch

Witch Island Brides:
The Vampire's Last Dance
The Wolf's New Year Bride
The Warlock's Enchanted Kiss
The Shifter's First Bite

Destiny Novels:
Defining Destiny
Accepting Fate

ABOUT THE AUTHOR

New York Times and USA Today bestselling author, Deanna Chase, is a native Californian, transplanted to the slower paced lifestyle of southeastern Louisiana. When she isn't writing, she is often goofing off with her husband in New Orleans or playing with her two shih tzu dogs. For more information and updates on newest releases visit her website at deannachase.com.

Made in the USA
Monee, IL
17 January 2021

57887766R00090